State College

at

Framingham

FOR LOVE OF A DOCTOR

Also by Elizabeth Seifert

Young Doctor Galahad
(*Winner of $10,000 Prize*)
A Great Day
Thus Doctor Mallory
Hillbilly Doctor
Bright Scalpel
Army Doctor
Surgeon in Charge
A Certain Doctor French
Bright Banners
Girl Intern
Doctor Ellison's Decision
Doctor Woodward's Ambition
Orchard Hill
Old Doc
Dusty Spring
So Young, So Fair
Take Three Doctors
The Glass and the Trumpet
The Strange Loyalty of
Dr. Carlisle
Hospital Zone
The Bright Coin
Homecoming
The Story of Andrea Fields
Miss Doctor
Doctor of Mercy
The Doctor Takes a Wife
The Doctor Disagrees
Lucinda Marries the Doctor
Doctor at the Crossroads
Marriage for Three
A Doctor in the Family
Challenge for Dr. Mays
A Doctor for Blue Jay Cove
A Call for Dr. Barton
Substitute Doctor
The Doctor's Husband
The New Doctor
Love Calls the Doctor
Home-Town Doctor
Doctor on Trial
When Doctors Marry
The Doctor's Bride
The Doctor Makes a Choice
Dr. Jeremy's Wife
The Honor of Dr. Shelton
The Doctor's Strange Secret
Legacy for a Doctor
Dr. Scott, Surgeon on Call
Katie's Young Doctor
A Doctor Comes to Bayard
Doctor Samaritan
Ordeal of Three Doctors
Hegerty, M.D.
Pay the Doctor
The Rival Doctors
Doctor with a Mission
To Wed a Doctor
The Doctor's Confession
Bachelor Doctor

FOR LOVE OF A DOCTOR

Elizabeth Seifert

DODD, MEAD & COMPANY
NEW YORK

Library of Congress Catalog Card Number: 73-88068

Printed in the United States of America
by Vail-Ballou Press, Inc., Binghamton, N. Y.

FOR LOVE OF A DOCTOR

1

It was a quiet evening; scarcely a leaf moved, and there was a hush upon the sounds usually heard along the roadside. Ahead of the car the ground began to fall away, down, and down again, toward the river. The sky was prettily mottled with little shell-like clouds, some of them pink, edged with lavender. Against the blue, these colors were, said Connie, rather sentimental.

"We'd not admire them anywhere but in the sky at sunset," she told her husband.

"It's all right to be sentimental," he answered, his deep voice warm and comforting, "at this time of the evening, returning home after a journey."

Connie touched his coat sleeve, not for attention, but to reassure herself that he was there beside her, strong, warm, and real. "It was a good trip," she said softly, "though I like the coming home— Oh there it is!"

John Buell chuckled and slowed to make the turn into their own driveway. "Didn't you expect 'it' to be right there?" he asked.

"I'm glad to see it," she told him earnestly. "Drive slowly, will you? So I can look at it. It is so beautiful. . . ."

"And costs a thousand dollars a year to heat," said her husband.

Connie's eyes lifted to his face. "Do you mind so much?" she asked.

"Sure I mind. All those tonsillectomies it takes to pay the heat bill. . . ."

"Maybe we should remodel it."

"We did remodel it—after the big house burned."

"What did the big house cost to heat?"

"I wasn't old enough to know or care. But a bundle, I'd say."

There were smile crinkles at the corners of his eyes. Connie Buell contentedly gazed at the picture which her home made as they approached it. Built of red sandstone, the entrance and windows framed in white, the misty spell of evening lay upon it. The old stones, still moist from the afternoon's rain, glistened, and the grass gleamed, beaded with jewels.

This home where the Buells lived was an enormous structure. It first had been built as a barn and carriage house for the large estate which John Buell's grandfather had established eighty years ago. When the big house burned, it had been converted into a dwelling a hundred feet by thirty, making a house of grand design, with a thirty-five-foot living room, great reaches of unused space, and the enormous fuel bill. But the Buells loved it and would live nowhere else.

Built on a downward slope, the house had three levels. The lower level, at the back, looked down across three acres of meadowland to the lovely little river at the foot of the hill. The second floor was at grade level and contained most of the family living rooms. The third story contained two bedrooms and a bath, with the rest of that floor a vast and drafty emptiness. Connie called this space her seventy-five-foot haymow.

Before John had married, he and his two brothers, Beaumont and Birch, and Birch's wife, had lived in the house, with room enough for all. Now Connie, her two small children, John, and the servants found it easy and pleasant to fill the place with living and love.

"The children will be tired and sleepy," she murmured, gazing at each tree, each shrub. "They won't appreciate the honor that was done you. . . ."

They were returning from a meeting where her husband, Dr. John Grey Buell, had been honored in a medical way; Connie was very proud of the slender, sun-browned man beside her. "But not surprised," she had told him. A nurse before marrying him, she knew that he was a leader in his profession. A quiet man, he spoke with a drawl, was reserved in his humor and in his manner. He had watchful eyes that could quickly spark to attention, and a firmly set mouth that could quickly quirk into laughter or, as quickly, harden with anger and resolve.

Connie again touched his sleeve. "I am proud of you," she said. "And your neighbors, your family, your friends—they will be proud, too."

John said nothing. He was negotiating the drive around the corner of the house and down the hill to the garage at the rear. Cleve, the houseman, would be watching for them and be there to receive them, to take the bags, to say his usual word of welcome. John glanced up at the long gallery, thinking that the children might be there with Madie; they were not.

". . . for outstanding performance and developments in thoracic surgery," Connie was quoting the article in the local newspaper which they had bought and read when they stopped to eat before driving out into the county and home.

". . . married to the former Constance Rohmer," John's quiet voice drolly continued the quotation.

"They did mention me, didn't they?" said Connie, ready to open the car door, to jump out, say "Hi, Cleve" to the waiting servant, and then run into the house, anxious to see it again, to see her children.

With Cleve's dignified "Good evening, Mrs. Buell" reproachfully in her ears—she really should learn to act like the wife of a distinguished surgeon!—Connie scampered up the stairs. The children were waiting there with Madie, and she gathered them joyously into her arms. Watchful-waiting Grey, and round, blond-curled, laughing Corey—she hugged them warmly, kissed them, relishing the feel of their soft skin, their firm little bodies, the smell of their hair. "Oh," cried their mother, "am I glad to see you!"

"Then why did you go away?" asked Grey soberly. "You didn't have to leave your dear little children. Did you, Mommy?"

Connie laughed delightedly. "Sometime you try to be two places at once," she told her son. "Were they well, Madie?"

"Oh, yes, ma'am," said the young woman. "They slept well, ate well—I took them to Sunday school.

"Well, good for all of you!"

A child holding each hand, Connie let them guide her to their special "room." It was called, in this house, the family room. John had definite ideas about preserving a certain part of his home for adult living, though three-quarters of the big house was devoted to the children. This end of the second-level floor was entirely designed for, and used by, Grey and Corey, and their parents functioning as such, Madie, the pretty, soft-spoken young woman who cared for the babies, a chow dog, two Siamese cats, and Emma and Cleve, the couple who "did for" the John Buells.

Cleve, a dignified man of sixty, wearing his white, starched jacket—he marked the event of evening by changing from a gray cotton jacket to this white one—was bringing up the bags, and now John was being greeted by the children, who were going through their usual noisy ritual of exploring his pockets to see what he had brought them.

For a minute, Connie stood watching them. "John does love his children," her mind told her. She looked about the family room—tiled floor, sturdy furniture, the view out across the river valley now almost obscured by mist and darkness.

The children came back to her, catching at her hands, touching her to be sure she was at home again. They adored their pretty young mother, and she was good to them, with them. She was always gay for them, as she was, usually, gay with all people, a friendly person. Connie liked to have fun, and did have fun.

"I'll put them to bed," she told Madie. "You deserve an evening off."

"If you're tired . . ." said Madie.

"Not that kind of tired. Just let me change out of my suit."

"Yes, ma'am."

Almost at once, Connie was back, her soft suit exchanged for a sleeveless dress of blue denim, her dark hair a cloud about her face.

Madie had the bath half filled with warm water—the children would go in together, though Grey was beginning to assert his right to privacy. Not tonight. Glad and relieved to have his mother home again, he reverted to a habit formed when he was two, but not used for months lately, of shucking out of his clothes, to run, naked and screaming with laughter, through the family room, slithering under his bed, darting into Corey's room, then back again, to be caught finally in the big upholstered armchair, to squeal and bounce, and cling to Connie when she carried him, laughing as hard as he could, to the bathtub where Corey was carefully soaping the washcloth and polishing the tiles.

"He's too heavy for you to carry," said John's voice from the doorway.

Connie looked over her shoulder at him. "I know," she said. "And he knows it, too. But tonight—he's glad to have me home. He thought perhaps I had deserted him."

"I'm glad you didn't bring home another baby," said Grey flatly. He took the washcloth away from Corey. She puckered up but accepted the sponge which Connie offered her as consolation. She was a sunny child, not easily upset.

"Wouldn't you be glad to have another baby?" Connie asked her son.

"For now I like it better this way," said Grey, sounding so much like John that even his father laughed.

The bath was accomplished with much hilarity and dampening of Connie's dress and hair. Sleepers were put on, prayers said, interrupted by Corey's description of a picnic which Madie had arranged.

"We just ate lunch out on the grass," Grey cut this down to reality.

"Picnic?" asked Corey, who was only two, and realized the limits of her vocabulary.

"Of course it was a picnic, darling," said Connie, hugging the child. "Now, let's start over. . . ."

Into their beds, then, Grey declaring that he was old

enough to climb in by himself. "I'm *four!*" he announced truculently.

Finally, night lights gleaming softly, Connie could say good night at each bedroom doorway, and go back across to change her dress again. She was a *mess!* But, oh, she did love to get into this kind of mess; she did love being the children's mother and, she told herself softly, being John's wife.

Here in their bedroom—a large room, with a soft green carpet, blue and green flowered curtains, a huge bed, already turned down for the night . . .

"John's wife," Connie whispered softly, taking a white dress from the closet, stepping out of the damp denim, carrying it to the hamper in the bathroom. Here in this room, where she would sleep with John that night, and every night, she knew what it was to be this man's wife, and to love him.

When she leaned forward to the mirror to put on fresh lipstick, she saw the smile of pride in her eyes. Well, she was proud. Happy. Glad. All the good words.

The white dress, slim pumps—she was ready to go on to the great living room where John would be waiting for her to fix him a drink. He looked up, smiling, when she came in, and he watched her as she set out the glass, tinkled the ice into it, carefully poured. . . .

As much as their bedroom, Connie felt that this bright room was the expression of her marriage. It was a casual room, designed for adults, for grown-up entertaining, for mature people relaxing and enjoying each other. It was a big room, thirty-five feet long, lending itself to several pleasant areas. Informal groups could gather about the huge fireplace, sit in the big square armchairs, on the orange and yellow and white upholstered couch, or bring up the ottomans to close the circle before the stone hearth.

In front of the sliding glass doors that opened upon the deck was a small game table with chairs about it for card playing or talking. At the far end of the room was a spot for reading; book-filled shelves extended from floor to ceiling; between them was a long slab desk and an orange-covered couch asking one to curl up and knit, listen to music, or stretch out full length, as John was doing that evening while he watched his wife fix him a drink.

His wife Connie. Constance. She was a small girl, and curvaceous, though as slender as a length of willow down by the river.

Pretty. Her cheekbones were high; her eyes were misty-blue—as blue and wide as Grey's—set a bit slantingly into her face. She had black hair, masses of it, cut and controlled into a soft frame for her face; her throat was slender, her bosom lifted like that of a young girl. A lovely line formed itself from shoulder to thigh, to waist. She was a lovely young woman.

And a capable, swiftly efficient one, too, who, Dr. Buell knew, could play poker until two in the morning, and be ready to administer spinal anesthesia at dawn. She was a matter-of-fact person, facing life as it came, always treasuring the high spots. She was gay with her children, and with her husband. Swiftly tender, but always with a certain withdrawal, a withholding, as if she were afraid to take, to handle, the full measure of life and love.

She was happy to be back in her home this night, and she must check on each thing, not take for granted that all would be as she had left it. She could bring John his drink, but she must wait to see if he still enjoyed it as she had learned from practice to mix it. She must be reassured; she must have some small coin of wealth to tuck away into her store of happy things. Later she could take these pennies out, examine them, and treasure them anew. "The children missed me," she could say. "They were happy to have me come home." "John waited for me to make his drink; he enjoyed it."

John recognized this need in Connie. So long as her store of treasure grew, she felt secure in their marriage. He had always felt sure of it; it was Connie who had felt it necessary to work at her happiness. That was not necessary, but—

He pointed to the mail on the desk. "You'll have a great time going through that," he said wryly.

"I'm glad you get your stuff at the office," she agreed. "Was there anything . . . ?"

"I opened only one or two. One important-looking letter announced a showing of furs."

She laughed. "There are things that interest me more." But she went over to the stack of mail, spread the envelopes into a fan on the desktop. John, his drink in his hand, picked up the telephone and dialed the hospital. His eyes watched Connie; now she was opening an envelope or two. He got the surgical floor and asked for his next day's schedule.

He was a tall man, John Grey Buell, with the strong shoulders and arms which a surgeon needs; his skin was smooth, and browner than most doctors usually show. For this Connie took credit. She, by her own admission, nagged her husband to get out of doors, if only to lie in the sun for an hour on their upper deck. This she insisted upon, winter and summer. As a result, John had a healthy color. His hair was brown and thick, his eyes, too, were brown, keen, and ready enough to smile. The hand which held his glass set it down so that he could make some notes on the pad beside the phone. His hands had, during the past week away from the scrub sinks, lost a little of their pink softness and looked only strong and capable. His waist was flat, his hips slim, his legs long and straight.

Connie, reading a note of thanks for a wedding gift, furtively watched him, telling herself again—for the thousandth time—how lucky she was to be this man's wife. She knew that she loved him, and would have loved him, married to him or not. But she was his wife, and so had been privileged to love him entirely—so entirely that after five years she felt herself to be an inner part of him. She felt as John Buell felt. When he picked up his glass, her own fingers knew the smooth curve of the glass; *she* could smell the mint, the perfume of the rum; her own tongue tasted the cold liquid.

She dropped the letters back to the desk, and as she turned away from it, she executed a little pirouette of exaltation. She moved about the room, touching things—a book on the shelf, the pillow where John had rested, the daisies in the vase on the table before the couch, the keystone of the fireplace arch. This was her home, and she loved it.

John watched her; he knew how Connie felt about her home, about her family. When he put the telephone down and tore off the memo sheet, he teased her gently. "You make a ritual of coming home," he told her. "Who was the goddess of the home? Her name surely was Constance. What happens if you find something gone or broken?"

She came to him, her dark-lashed eyes wide and solemn. "You don't know what it means to me," she said earnestly.

John's gaze went briefly beyond her head to a movement on the gallery; Connie did not notice. "If things get broken," she said, still in that gravely intent voice, "I make a note of it. I keep a sort of bookkeeping record. You brought me that little cup and saucer from France two years ago. It added to my riches. If it should be broken, I would know a loss. Is that wrong, John, to feel so?"

"Nothing you ever do or say is wrong," her husband assured her. "Hello, Birch."

Connie turned swiftly; she had not seen Birch on the deck; she had not heard the door slide open—he must have been there long enough to hear what she had said and to see her tense earnestness.

He came across the room and lightly touched her shoulder. "It's your hungry past that makes you hoard things," he told John's wife. "How are you both? It's good to have you home again."

Feeling her cheeks burn, and not wanting Birch to see the flush, nor John, Connie said something about checking on the children—Madie was not there—and left the room.

When she came back, to the bedroom, not the living room, she could hear Birch and John talking earnestly. As she unpacked their bags and moved about the bedroom, she could hear the brothers' deep voices rumbling along, sometimes rising into recognizable words. She liked Birch Buell, for all his teasing. He was a very big man, a very good man, and gentle. Three years younger than John, Birch's hair had turned white at the temples. That, with his hairline mustache, made him more handsome than John. Or perhaps he would seem so to other women. Not to Connie.

Finally, and not too soon, Connie thought—John had a full day tomorrow, and was surely tired from the trip—she heard movement in the living room to indicate that Birch was leaving. "Where did Connie get to?" she heard him ask. He said something else, and John said, "Leave the girl alone."

"Is she p.g. again?" asked her brother-in-law.

"No," said John. "Oh, she may be—but don't tease her, Birch. She doesn't like it—and she's a fine girl; we want to keep her that way."

"She *is* a fine girl," said Birch heartily. "And a feast for the eyes as well. Whatever made me think I wanted to marry a redhead? Connie's much prettier. Whatever her past, her present couldn't be lovelier."

John said something about not talking about that, either. "You know your remarks will certainly reach Irene."

"About Connie's past?" Connie could imagine how innocent Birch would be looking.

"No!" cried John. "She doesn't have any *past*. Not one that matters. But your wife would not appreciate your remarks on Connie's looks."

"I guess you're right," Connie heard Birch say. Then she heard his feet on the deck and on the outside stairs. From the foot of them he would cut down the hill to his home.

2

But the "past" did matter to Connie Buell. Somehow Birch had discovered that it did, without knowing much of anything about her past. He didn't really think that she had a lurid one, but he liked to tease, and see her blush prettily with confusion. Connie knew that was all there was to it. But—still—

Her "past" had not been, entirely, a hungry one. Connie's family was of the decent middle class. Her father was a pharmacist, her mother sang in the church choir. They had when she was a child, a girl; they were being and doing those things now.

Connie had grown up in their small, midwest town—not as small as some, but certainly not a city in the true sense. She had been pretty as a child, and when she reached high school, she found herself popular. She was chosen for the right clubs and societies; she was invited to the dances; she went to basketball games, to football games, to picnics in the summer, on hayrides . . . She was having a wonderful time. She looked forward to having an even more wonderful time when she would finish high school and go on to one of the state colleges or maybe even to the University. No one asked, too seriously, what Connie Rohmer wanted "to be." As pretty as she was, and as nice, they knew what lay ahead for Connie. College, a romance, a pretty wedding. She dreamed of those things herself, not in any special hurry to have them happen.

Then—toward the end of her junior year, before she was quite seventeen, romance of a sort came to Connie. It was a grubby romance, though it did not seem so to the starry-eyed girl she was at that time.

The man was the new science teacher at the high school. He had arrived that fall, and all the girls immediately swooned over him. He was enough older than those girls to make the high school boys seem all legs, arms, and hooting voices. This fellow was handsome. At that time of crew cuts, on a rainy day his hair would knot into tight curls. His good looks were of the strong, virile type. His eyes were knowing, and sparkled with mischief. He had a way of saying unexpected, and startling, things. There was an intriguing scar up against his hairline. He made a thing of telling how he had acquired it, the stories different each time, and all outrageous—either impossibly heroic or ridiculously funny.

"In the Korean bit, I threw myself on a land mine, saved the general's life. I got blown to bits, but this is all you can see of the damage."

Or—"I caught my foot in a climbing rope at the gym. The damn thing swung back and forth—*swang?*—and rubbed this place on my head."

Nobody believed his stories, nor cared. This big man was a stranger in town, in the school community where everyone had known everyone for years. He was exciting.The high school girls all vied for the new teacher's interest, and when it became evident that Connie Rohmer was in the lead for his favor, the other girls shivered with vicarious thrill and questioned her endlessly. What did he say? What did he wear? What did he do? Where did you go? How did you feel . . . ?

Almost fifteen years later, Connie well remembered those sessions. She could place her friends, see what they were wearing, hear their voices, see their round, avid eyes. In the gym locker room, at the drugstore huddled over milk shakes and Cokes, in her room at home . . .

"What did you *do?*"

"And then what did you do?"

By late spring her father began to be disturbed, and finally he objected to her seeing Scottie. He was too old, he told his daughter. She should date boys her own age. "Or try staying at home for a change. Who knows? You might like it."

When her response had been stubborn, even sullen, he had suspected plans to see Scottie, whether on a "date" or not.

"You might tell this professor," her father had said then, "that if he persists in hanging around you, I'll go to the school board."

In those days that was more of a threat than it came to be later. In any case, it frightened Connie, and she told Scottie that she should not see him, "except in class, of course."

He had laughed, but she had insisted that her father was entirely serious. She would not plan on any dates—no, she would not go for a drive to talk things over. Oh, he must not think of coming to the house or of talking to her father anywhere!

But there did come a day—just a week before the end of school—the junior class was giving its annual picnic for the graduating seniors. The faculty were invited, and Scottie came. The picnic was held on a grassy stretch before a sandstone cliff. There was a pool of water, green and cold. "Bottomless," it was said to be. There were tall trees, and interesting paths back into the woodland.

Not entirely against her will—her better judgment did not enter into the matter—Connie let Scottie entice her into a stroll away from the others. They were not the only strolling couple. But since he was a teacher, their departure must have been noted by everyone.

Connie remembered exactly what she had worn—a dark blue skirt and a sleeveless blouse of pale pink cotton. A pink ribbon was tied around her dark hair; she wore canvas slippers.

It was wonderful to be with Scottie, and after they got into the woods, she let him hold her hand. His hand fondled her bare arm, and then he drew her to him; he embraced her and kissed her. Hard. So hard that he frightened her.

"You've not let a man kiss you before?" he asked her.

"Well, of course I've been kissed!" She dabbed at her lips, which felt bruised.

He pulled her toward him again and kissed her again. He could not lose her, he said; he would not lose her.

Connie was only sixteen, but she thought that she was a woman. Her body had misled her. And she did not protest to any effect when Scottie led her to where he had left his car at the side of the road, away from the picnic grounds and the other cars. In a haze of excitement and embarrassed joy, she got in and said, yes, they could drive—a little way—

It was an old car, but it swiftly took them away from the high school group and from the town. When Scottie stopped for gas, Connie said they should turn back; it was getting late.

"We're not going back," he told her.

She could only stare at him.

"That's right," he said. "We are running away."

She didn't want to run away. She felt sure that she loved Scottie—he could make shivers run through her limbs and along her spine—and—

They drove for hours and hours. Scottie would not listen to her doubts and objections. He told her that everything would be wonderful; she would see. Now and then he would touch her in a way that both frightened her and thrilled her.

They drove across the river and through the mountains, and finally—at midnight—Scottie told her they were in Arkansas. "We can be married here," he said. "And no questions asked."

Married! The thought had not come to the girl. But Scottie laughed at her again. He was not about to run away with her and not marry her, he declared.

Her own timidity, her fright, her innocence were as much to blame as Scottie's bravado. They found the home of the justice of the peace. A constable on a lonely street in a lonely town told them leeringly where to go.

"Lots of people come across the state line," Scottie told her.

She barely remembered that wedding. There was a porch across the front of the small house. It took a time to rouse the old man and his wife. They knew at once what was wanted. And almost at once, she and Scottie were married. They signed a paper, Scottie gave the justice some money, and they were back in the car, Scottie's hands ever more bold upon her young body.

They spent their wedding night in a small-town hotel; the sheets of the bed were of unbleached muslin, seamed down the middle, and rough to the skin. Scottie was tempestuous, and laughed loudly. The young girl had not expected love to be as it was.

The next morning they ate breakfast at a long table where other inmates of the hotel looked at them knowingly and sniggered. Cold canned tomatoes featured that breakfast, and soggy fried potatoes.

Scottie had apologized for the hotel and the breakfast. "We'll do better," he promised. "Though I have to watch my money. But we'll go to the city, and I'll get a job."

The city they went to was Memphis.

But in Memphis, Scottie did not find a job. He and Connie lived in a single room in a shabby, crowded part of town. Their love in that room was grubby, their life was grubby. Within a week Connie could not find any trace of the Scottie, the "older man" whose touch and kiss and presence once had thrilled her.

After a month they had no money, and Scottie still could not find a job. He said he could not give his teaching position as reference for a good job, and he had a rheumatic heart, which would not let him do hard labor. Connie would not listen to his suggestion that she ask her father for help.

They quarreled about this. They fought, really. Connie was frightened, shamed, and for the first time in her life, hungry. In those two months she grew up fast.

At the end of them she got herself a job, of sorts, in a dime store. This, at least, would let them eat frugally and rent a room in an even grubbier part of town.

It was close to Christmas of that same year—she was homesick and tired from the overtime hours she was putting in—that she came home to find Scottie gone. He was not in the room when she arrived; he did not come in during the night. Next day she went to work, and on her return she did not find that he had been home during the day.

She did not worry. Her relief at being alone both shamed her and encouraged her. If he had deserted her— She waited for a month before she would let herself be sure. She went along as she was, where she was, working by day and by night relishing her own individuality again. It was February before she began to make any plans. She had no friends. She had always been a popular girl, with family and friends about her, but now she did not want to be with people. Except for her work, she saw no one. She did not want to continue as a dime-store clerk; she vaguely thought about going home, but pride always interrupted such thinking.

She did not want to stay where she was. By then she was ready to acknowledge that she hated and feared Scottie Stringer, and that she was terrified by the thought of his possible return.

So she moved to a different room, and she got a different job. She began to save some money, slowly, painfully. In the summer, she left Memphis, moving, by stages, as far as Cleveland.

It was there that she got a job as an aide, and then as an assistant in the laboratories, of a large medical center. She found sanctuary in the big buildings. She liked the work she did, and took pride in it. She wanted to learn. In the evening she attended classes, and attained her high school diploma. She still did not want to be with people, but because of the work, which she did want to do, and well, she had to learn to live with them—not to withdraw visibly from them. This accomplished, she learned to accept the presence of others about her. She still did not make close friends; she would not accept any dates, but she did become more friendly. She called herself Constance Rohmer, finding that the name went far toward restoring her own identity. When she got some money ahead, she would get a divorce. But she moved slowly, holding on to each thing she gained, fiercely wanting to keep it and protect it

She had to look well at work; she began to dress better away from work, always mindful of cost. She was living in a hotel for women, comfortable and protected. She could begin to think that life might hold something ahead for her.

And then, one day, a detail man—a salesman for a drug firm—showed up in the lab. He was a friendly chap; he passed out compliments to the lab girls, breath mints, and offers of a chance to have coffee with him. When he came up to Connie, a girl new to him, and looked at her small, dark-haired person bent over a microscope, he frowned. He walked around the bench and leaned over in an effort to see her face. "Connie?" he said then.

She looked up. Few people now called her Connie.

"I thought I knew you!" cried the young man. "You're Connie Rohmer. I know your father. I've been in his drugstore every two months for five years."

He did know her, of course. And Connie knew him. When he asked her to have dinner with him that evening, she hesitated—she wanted to hear about home, and her parents—but—

"Well, I know you can," said the pleasant young man. "I heard a year ago that the guy you eloped with was dead. Stringer. Wasn't that his name? Sure it was. Scottie . . ."

Connie sat stunned. If this were true . . . Oh, if it only *could* be true!

She must know more to be sure. They couldn't talk here in the lab. She said she would eat dinner with the detail man.

During the rest of the afternoon she thought about the possibilities. Scottie could be dead. He had a bad heart; he could have had an attack—sometime, somewhere— She had moved frequently, not leaving any forwarding address.

That evening she questioned the detail man for every item of information he could give her. When? Where?

Who had told him that Scottie was dead?

"Why," said her host, "I believe that your father told me. Oh, it was maybe a year ago. Six months at least. It's too bad, of course."

Connie took a deep breath. "Yes." she said. "It was—it is too bad."

But, at last she was free—and relieved beyond belief.

Now she could make a life for herself, and live it in reality. She could plan, and do—

The next day at the hospital she asked about nurse's training; she was nineteen years old.

That night she wrote a letter to her parents, telling them where she was and what she planned to do. It was a difficult letter to write; she made a half-dozen attempts.

It was also a letter difficult to receive and read in the home where she had lived as a child and young girl, a home which she had left, it seemed, without a turn of her head.

Within a matter of days, she had a reply. Her parents were glad to hear from her; they had been wishing, praying, to hear. They loved her. Would she come home and let them help her do the things she wanted to do?

Her doubt of human relationships made her hesitate. She could manage alone, and would—

But she did go home.

The return had been an emotional experience. Nothing seemed to have changed except Connie. Her clothes still hung in the closet of her room; her parents looked the same. But the young girl had become a woman, grave-eyed, sweet, and quiet.

She was glad to be at home, but she said she did not want to see people. Her parents agreed. Her father made a request on his own part. He called it an injunction. "We are never to speak of Stringer!" he said sternly. "Never! He is dead. Let him stay that way."

He did, however, show Connie an article which he had clipped from the local newspaper. It told that Scottie had been killed in an automobile accident south of St. Louis. It gave the time, the place. And the concluding paragraph told that Scott Stringer had been a former teacher in the local high school. He had married Constance Rohmer. . . .

Connie sat holding the bit of newspaper in her hands. This had happened a month after she left Memphis. She—

"Let him be dead," said her father softly. "Will you promise not to speak of him? In time, you will not think of him."

But of course she would think of him—against her will, in her dreams at night—the sound of his voice, the touch of his hands, the very smell of him—the shameful memory of her own response to him.

"I'll promise not to speak of him," she told her father. "I'll be glad not to."

"All right," said her good father. "Then we can all start new."

A week later she returned to Cleveland. When a new class was formed in the Nursing School, Constance Rohmer was a member of it, a pretty, quiet, dark-haired girl. Her blue dress and white apron were becoming to her, as was her cap when she earned it. She liked the work, and her relief from worry about Scottie let her somewhat relax her wariness about people. A sparkle returned to her eyes, and a lilt to her voice. She worked hard and graduated when she was twenty-two, such a pretty young woman that men were a problem, but one which she felt quite capable of handling. By now she knew that men were not the prize packages they thought they were and that most women thought they were.

Then—this was seven years ago, when Connie was twenty-five—she met Beeze Buell. Beaumont Beaudelaire Buell, no less, or so his chart read that morning when Connie Rohmer came on duty. He had been hurt in an automobile accident; along with various bruises and abrasions, he had a badly broken leg. He was in a private room, with his own nurses assigned. He had been cared for during the night. Miss Rohmer was not his nurse, but she was o.r. head, and as was her practice with all post-operative patients, she went in to speak to Mr. Buell. She found him a pleasant young man with sun-browned skin, black hair close to his skull, and good eyes. He was uncomfortable in the fracture frame, but in no danger. On her first visit he made Connie laugh. Mainly about his name. No one ever called him anything but Beeze, he told the pretty young woman, crisp in her whites.

Connie liked him. Before she left his room, she read his chart more carefully. Beaumont Beaudelaire Buell was twenty-eight years old, his next of kin was a brother, Dr. John Buell. So he was not married. . . . The private room said money. "Beeze" was an architect.

Later that day his brother arrived—Dr. John Buell. Because he was a doctor, a surgeon, he was especially welcomed in the hospital. Because she was o.r. head, when he was taken around, Miss Rohmer met him, and liked him. He was a quieter man than his younger brother. It was difficult now for

Connie to think about John as he was when she first had seen him. Slender, dark, quiet—a handsome man, with eyes like his brother's—the hospital doctors all spoke well of him as a rapidly rising chest surgeon. Connie had immediately liked him as a man.

Satisfied as to his brother's condition and care, Dr. Buell had departed. At the end of the next week he returned for a two-day visit. By then Beeze had well established himself on the surgical floor. He was a mischievous man, he could be brusque, even devastating—and he could be romantic, too—all of which took doing for a man in such a fracture frame. But Beeze managed it. He had been struck by the pretty Operating Head, and often asked for her. The other nurses told Connie that he had; she fell into the habit of speaking to him as she passed his door, going into the room for a minute if she had time. Connie liked Beeze; she still liked him.

On the week end when John Buell returned to visit his brother, Connie—on call for o.r. duty—played poker with the two men and the intern, also on call. They had good fun and good talk. Beeze was not sick. He could play poker all night in his room if his companions were not noisy, if what they were doing did not disturb the rest of the hospital.

The game was good, and so was the talk. Connie and the intern kept their eyes and ears open, but said little. When they finally were called away, they mutually agreed that they liked the Buells, especially the doctor.

"Only because of his profession and ours," Connie had specified.

"Well, sure," said the intern. "I'd like to work with him, wouldn't you?"

"Yes, I would," said Connie.

Beeze Buell was in traction for six weeks, and on four of those week ends his brother flew in to be with him. Other friends came, and another brother, but Connie only heard about them. She always saw Dr. Buell. The hospital asked him to consult on various cases, and twice he operated. He was an excellent surgeon, Connie knew. He was unmarried, too. He thought Connie was his brother's girl, so he was no more than friendly to the pretty nurse, but even John's friendliness . . .

Connie fell head over heels in love with the man. This time it was love, she was dismayed to acknowledge. She had vowed that no man would again—ever—reach her that way. She was fairly safe, of course, because Dr. Buell was ready only to be courteous to her. But she . . .

Good heavens! The wakeful nights, the periods of daytime dreaming, the quickened pulse, the tingles and prickles— She hated to see him leave; she looked forward to his return—

Beeze detected how things were for Connie, and he gave his brother a push. Later John told Connie about it. He had not only been willing, he was delighted. He had thought the nurse was Beeze's girl.

"Not after you showed up," Beeze had said. "But I can help your cause along."

"You can keep yourself out of it, if you please!" retorted his brother. "I'll do my own courting."

"Then get about it, will you?" Beeze advised. "I'll not be trussed up here forever."

A year later—so long because of Connie's fears and doubts —she and John were married, with all of her doubts immediately stilled. Marriage to this man was wonderful from the first.

Their wedding was a small one, in her parents' home. John's brothers had attended, and when the couple returned to John's home, the bride was dismayed to find that the brothers lived in the house with him, and were prepared to live there with the bride.

This was more than she had bargained for, and Connie was unable to conceal her dismay. The brothers made no secret of their amusement at her reaction.

Beeze said that he had stayed on only "to see her face." He already had rented and furnished an apartment in the city. His consideration for Connie, his admiration, had persisted.

But Birch—he made John ask him and Irene to leave. This was Irene's fault, Connie always had thought. She did not want to leave the large home; she had been the first bride to come to it and to run it. It was their home. John and his wife were welcome to stay, she said—for a time, at least.

But John was the oldest brother. The house had been willed to him if he wanted to live in it. It seemed that he did want to. And Birch moved Irene out. They went first to live in a hotel while the old tenant house on the Buell property was rebuilt and furnished for them. Irene had not liked doing any of this. Birch had been gentle with her, but firm. The tenant cottage made an attractive home.

Irene thought Birch should have rebuilt the "big house" which had burned to the ground ten years before. The big house, John told Connie, would never be rebuilt. He talked about making a swimming pool out of the old cellar hole, but when they did put in a pool, it was closer to their house. That house itself had undergone some changes after their marriage. It was too big, but both Connie and John enjoyed it. The children's coming justified their claiming it.

Birch and Irene had no children. There were various things that were not right in Birch's marriage—things other than Irene's open dislike of Connie, which used to worry her. It no longer did.

3

THINGS WERE very right indeed with Connie Buell and her marriage. She still had her reserves, but John was the sort of man to respect her need for them, and to take the happiness which was his in his wife, his home, and his family. He adored his two children, and was sure of his wife's happiness. And of course she was happy. She had in her life everything she had ever wanted, everything any woman could want.

She had never told John anything about Scottie. It was the only deceit she had practiced with him. But she *had* to! Scottie was dead, and that shabby affair need have no part in her present life.

In the first year or so of her marriage to John, she had felt some doubts about not talking freely to him of the past. She thought a wife should have no secrets from her husband. But the matter did not seem to disturb John. They both lived in the happy present.

Literally, the past seemed to be dead, and the busyness of her present life proved, to her at least, that one could and should go on with living as best one could, and as happily.

Connie was busy. The big house and the grounds took managing. Madie was a competent nursemaid for the children, and Cleve and Emma did the physical work of the house. George, the yardman, cared for the grounds.

Because of her nurse's training, Connie made herself useful in the community. She served at health clinics; she gave one afternoon a week to a rehabilitation center. John's position in the community and the medical world entailed various social duties for his wife. Connie learned to entertain in their home; she gladly went with John to dinners, concerts, the theater.

She learned to play a good hand of bridge, and to handle the matter—difficult for her—of small talk. They belonged to a country club, but Connie shook her head at any suggestion of golf. She could swim, and did. She tried to learn tennis, but she was not good at it. However, she was very good at croquet, as she always pointed out, and the brothers installed a croquet court at the "house," where cutthroat games were played.

She never let herself get so busy that she could not give her children hours of her time. She did as well as a companion for her husband.

Hers may not have been a perfect marriage—if such existed—but it was a good one, certainly.

All these things, these memories, these sadnesses and happinesses, passed through Connie's mind that evening like a swift reel of film. Her husband and his brother talked together in the living room, and she welcomed the chance to check on her home. She unpacked their clothes—hers and John's—cherishing the intimacy of handling his possessions as if they were her own. They *were* her own! The little leather case of studs and cuff links, the rumpled handkerchiefs which he had used—all to be sorted and placed into drawer, hamper, or on a pile of clothing to be sent to the cleaner.

She went across to the children's wing and checked on those possessions with much the same feeling of warm pleasure and security. These things, these babies, John had given her. She smoothed Corey's hair back from her brow, and straightened the tumbled sheet and blanket on Grey's bed—he was a thrasher and a turner!

She went to the kitchen and the pantry and checked on the food supplies, the plans for the next day. She told Emma about the laundry and the things for the cleaner. She talked to her and Cleve a little about their trip, the things they had seen and done.

She went downstairs to the stoop, the stone-paved area below the sheltering balcony. This was a quiet place by night, a secure place. One could, in the darkness, hear the faint lap of water in the swimming pool. One could smell the fragrance of the roses coming into full bloom and the perfume of newly cut grass.

She went up to her bedroom again, in time to hear Birch's departing word; she joined the men in time to say good night to him.

As they went back into the living room, John looked at her inquiringly. Had she been miffed, or only tactful, he asked, taking the used glasses over to the tray.

Connie shook her head. "Neither one," she told him. "I was just checking the twigs in the nest."

John chuckled and picked up a magazine.

"You should go to bed," his wife told him. "From what I heard of your call, it sounded as if tomorrow's schedule would be a heavy one."

"I expected it to be. All scheduled at the one hospital, however."

"Things pile up, I know."

"But it's been a good week."

"Ye-es," said Connie.

He put the magazine down and came to her. His fingertips lifted her chin so that he could look into her eyes. "Wasn't it good, Connie?" he asked, his voice deep.

"Oh, yes!" she said quickly. "It was fine."

She would have turned away, but his hand on her shoulder held her where she was. His eyes searched her face. "Are you letting Birch bother you?" he asked.

"In what way?"

"I think you may have overheard—he was only teasing. He, too, thought you could overhear."

"I did hear what he said about my being pregnant. Since that's none of his business, I was not bothered. But, John—whatever he said—perhaps when I couldn't overhear—does seem to have bothered you."

John released her. "No," he said thoughtfully. "I was not bothered by anything he said to you, or about you. But the guy seems to have his own troubles."

"Oh, dear." Of course Birch had troubles. Connie did not like Irene; she had never liked her. She knew it, and wished she need not be with the woman, even in a discussion of her, and Birch.

She turned off one big lamp and another; she moved to the glass doors, meaning to lock them. She spoke of the children. "I told Emma we'd see to things in here," she said. "That we were going to bed as early as we could."

John watched her, understanding her reluctance to talk about Birch—or, rather, about Irene. He followed her into the bedroom; there the lamps glowed softly beside the bed and beside his armchair. He walked to the glass door and held out his hand to Connie. Together they stepped out on the balcony. Behind them the lighted room was like a picture of beauty and warmth—quiet.

A small breeze blew their hair, and John drew Connie into the circle of his arm, against the warmth and shelter of his body. They stood so, gazing out across the valley; the river gleamed softly in the starlight, the trees blew in a changing pattern against the sky.

Yang; the dog, a chow, barked twice.

"He's testing his vocal cords," said John, laughing. There was no other sound except those always heard, and so unheard, of distant road travel, a plane high overhead. . . .

"I'm afraid," said John, "that we are going to have to stand by Birch in this trouble of his." His hand warmed the bare curve of her shoulder and arm.

"Yes," murmured Connie. "You're his brother. . . ."

"There's more to it than that, sweetheart. Birch is a good man, married to a bitch."

Connie was so startled that she jerked, and his grasp tightened. "Oh, John," she breathed in soft protest.

"She is one!" he insisted.

"I know," said Connie, "but is it for you to say so?"

"I said much more than that to Birch tonight."

"Dear—"

"I told him to divorce the woman. And be quick about it."

"John," said Connie, troubled. In the faint light, she could see how stern her husband was looking. "In a thing like this, don't you think we—you—should stay out?" She didn't know what the "thing" was, but she could guess.

"Why should I stay out?" John asked. "You just reminded me he is my brother."

"Yes, he is. And old enough, isn't he, to decide things for himself?"

He turned to the glass doors. "Let's go inside," he said gruffly. "It's getting too cool out here."

They went in and began their preparations for bed. Six years of marriage had taught them how to proceed, and not interfere one with the other.

Connie undressed and put on robe and slippers, then laid things out for the morning, John's clothes and hers. John shed his garments as he crossed the room, picked up his pajamas, and—

"He brought the subject to me," he told his wife.

Connie unbuttoned the fresh shirt. "You could have listened to all he had to say, but—" She hung the shirt on the mahogany rack and turned to look at John. "Would you let Birch tell you what to do about your life, about me?"

"If I needed that sort of help, yes, I would talk to him." He went into the bathroom.

Connie pressed her lips to gether. She sincerely hoped the matter would never come up.

She finished her preparations for bed while John showered. For a good five minutes, the water roared and splashed, and the big bathroom became filled with steam. In the morning he would shower again, with cold water. Connie preferred the sunken tub, her bath taken in a leisurely fashion before she dressed.

She was still sitting before the dressing table when he came out of the stall, wielding the big towel vigorously. "Birch has already told Irene that he wants a divorce," he said.

"Oh, dear," murmured Connie, getting up to go back to the bedroom.

"He knows," said John, following her, the blue pajama coat

in his hands, "that she gives him every ground he needs—adultery, indignities—the works."

"I suppose the man would be Cliff Adams," said Connie softly.

"Of course it's Adams," said John loudly. "That man has been underfoot for a year. I don't know why Birch didn't punch him in the jaw months ago."

"How long have they been married?" asked Connie. "Eight years? Seven? Birch probably knows what results he'd get. I don't know Mr. Adams very well. I once met him at a party. He's a charmer."

"Oh, yes," growled John. "Boyish charm, outrageous things to say. Outrageous fun things to do. . . ."

He waited for Connie to get into bed, then he turned out the lights and joined her. His arm went under her shoulders, but he still wanted to talk.

"What did Irene say," Connie asked, "when he told her he wanted a divorce?"

"Birch said she laughed and called him old-fashioned."

"Oh, John."

"When Birch married her," said Birch's brother, "she was a stunning girl. Red hair, white skin—she danced like a professional. And of course Birch *is* old-fashioned. I am, too."

Connie rolled her head on his shoulder and caressed his hand. John was gentle, sweet—a big man, a clever doctor—and he played things straight. She tried to put all these adjectives to Birch, and, yes, so far as she knew, they applied.

"Your parents must have raised their sons . . ." she said sleepily. "Did Birch come up here tonight to ask you if he was old-fashioned?"

She could feel his almost-silent laughter. Lying so closely against each other, once Connie had told John he could not change his mind in the night without her knowing it.

"You know Birch, don't you?" he asked her now. "Yes, that is what he asked me."

"And . . . ?" murmured his wife, hoping that he would soon go to sleep. He would be up before seven, off and away to the hospital—one of the hospitals where he was a staff surgeon. His day would be long, and full. Surgery, consultations, examinations—catching up on post- and pre-operative cases. . . .

"I pointed out to Birch," said John, "that his trouble was not a matter of committed adultery."

Putting her hand on his strong, barrel-like chest, Connie raised herself, making an effort to see John's face. Her fingertip touched the corner of his eye. He caught at it with his hand and kissed it.

He had not been smiling; sometimes when he spoke gravely, a smile on his face would tell that he was joking. But tonight—

"Any marriage," he continued his discussion, "which can be broken by adultery—one side or the other doesn't matter—that marriage was on the rocks before the act. There was some great wrong in the situation between her and Birch, or Irene would not have *looked* at Adams."

He was right. Connie, since marrying John, had not "looked" at other men. "What did Birch say to that?" she asked.

"He said he would think it over."

"There's a lot to think about in that," said Connie. "When he came up here tonight—did he want to stay here? He could, you know. Not Irene. But Birch—"

"I believe now, looking over the whole thing, that he may have come up here with that idea in mind. But after we talked, he left. I expect he plans to make another try of talking to Irene. He's a lawyer, and he knows that a divorce often does not settle things."

"Their marriage *is* wrong . . ." Connie murmured, as if telling herself this long-acknowledged fact. Irene was self-centered, demanding—ruthless—

"It always was wrong," John agreed with her.

"Why?" asked Connie. "Why did they marry, I mean. If Birch has always been—what you called him—old-fashioned. Irene never was, was she?"

"She never was anything Birch was. But as to why they married —I could say it was just one of those things."

"I'd let you, if you'd stop there and go to sleep."

"I can't sleep with this on my mind, Connie."

No, he could not. "Then we'll talk it out."

For a long minute he was silent.

"It began about eight years ago," John said then. "Before I was lucky enough to know you. Before Beeze smashed up his leg. Irene was then working in a brokerage company. A good-looking girl. Strawberry blonde would be the term. She had been doing secretarial work for five years, and I don't believe a career had ever been in her plans. She was one of the bright, well-dressed young women one sees in the restaurants and bars about town."

"Did you know her?"

"By sight only. Doctors like me don't eat lunch downtown or stop for a martini after work."

"And that's where she met Birch?"

"Well, he did both things. He was, as he is now, a good-looking man; he was unmarried; he had some money, both through inheritance and his own efforts. He was a nice guy. Most people thought so. Girls—almost all the girls—made a fuss over him. So much so that I wondered if he would ever marry. Then Irene came along, saw him, met him—and she looked at him speculatively. She probably asked herself, as I understand a lot of young women do ask, 'Could I get this man?' She soon began to ask that question seriously about Birch, and to work on its answer. Her friends were marrying, and she probably felt that she might lose the boat. Miss it, I mean. So she intensified her efforts with Birch. She was a pretty woman to begin with—she really is, Connie."

"Yes," said Connie.

"Perhaps I am wrong. Perhaps she didn't manage anything. But in any case, Birch and she began to date. I don't know the details, really. But—quite soon, she managed an engagement. At least, they became engaged."

She managed it, thought Connie, knowing Irene.

"But I was there," said John, "and on the alert, when Cliff Adams entered the picture."

Connie's eyes widened. "Way back then?" she asked. "Before she married Birch?"

"Oh, yes. It was shortly before. Irene was going on a trip of some sort. I happened to take her to the plane. Birch was tied up and asked me to do it. I could and did manage. He was on a court case, something about the jury not coming in, as I remember. Anyway, that evening I drove Irene to the airport. There was some difficulty with the plane, and the pilot came into the boarding lounge to explain the delay, to apologize, to reassure the passengers that he would not depart unless everything was absolutely perfect.

"Cliff Adams was that pilot. As you say, a charmer. Red hair, freckles, an engaging grin—I suppose all the passengers found him attractive. He was entirely at ease, joking with the people, even saying a few shocking—or, well—provocative things. He was funny, too. I'll agree that he was. He talked to each person individually, but he rather lingered over Irene. She was, perhaps, the most attractive woman in the group—well-dressed and bright-mannered herself. There was the glamor of Adams' uniform, his wings, his job. He talked to me, but his eyes stayed on Irene. And when the plane took off, I was as sure as I am standing here—lying here—tonight that they would have a date at their destination. I had seen the spark between those two."

"Did you tell Birch?"

"I did not. Even then I was hoping that the incident meant Irene could, and would, ditch my brother."

"But she didn't."

"No. They went on and got married."

"Do you think Adams is more her sort?"

"I'd say so. And I think he has kept somewhat in touch with her, too. As for Birch, and her marriage—there have been seven years of their 'getting along.' I've felt sorry for Birch; I've resented Irene."

With cause, Connie knew. The matter of getting along—she knew about the quarrels, the pouting which Irene did to get her way, the undercurrents of resentment on both sides, though Birch exerted the most effort to make his marriage work. He was, generally, patiently enduring; he tried to please his wife—he usually would walk out on a quarrel. . . .

"Now do you think there is real trouble?" Connie asked.

"Now there seems to be trouble, and Birch thinks it is real. For the past year, Adams has been stationed here; this has been his home base. He has come to the house. Birch knows that. You've met him there. Irene sees him in various ways—and Birch has found that out. So he asked for a divorce, and she laughed at him."

"Called him old-fashioned," murmured Connie. "Maybe his talking to her will help."

"Maybe," said John. "I'm sorry for Birch. He's made a lot of his own trouble, but I do wish he could have been as lucky as I have been."

"Irene's the lucky one in that family," said Connie.

"I think it is fair to say that," John agreed. "Birch is all right."

In a few minutes he was asleep, breathing deeply. But Connie lay at his side, wide awake, again thinking of her own past in brief, shadowy detail. Her marriage to John—the day he asked her to marry him—the wedding, her first knowledge of what a man could be with the woman he loved. She thought, unwillingly, of Scottie and his brusque demands upon her, his taking without giving, his—

She thought of his rough, curly hair—marital intimacy had been a shock to the young girl and a joyless duty to the woman she had so quickly become. Scottie had demanded—taken—shamed—his bride. Deserting her had been his only gift to her.

It had not been a matter of money. Connie could imagine John under similar circumstances. She could, today, be poor with John. She would gladly work for him, scrub and clean, and go gladly, warmly, into his embrace. There would be none of the ugliness which she had known with Scottie. Against her will she remembered *his* embrace; she shuddered to think back to the rooms where they had lived, the smell of them—dampness and cooking smells, the old dirt in the crevices, the bugs—the noises—but above all, the inescapable intimacy with a man she did not love.

Years after she was free of him, Connie had read something from Mark Twain. "One's intimacies either refine or corrupt," he had written. Connie knew that was true!

Her whole experience with Scottie had been marked by corruption. John—her soft arms hugged her love for him against her breast, holding that love close, wanting to shut out even her memory of what life had been with Scottie Stringer.

It made her sick, even today, to remember her months with him. She wished she could put it all behind her, and usually she did—by keeping busy, by living the life which John had given her. She relished that life. Her big, lovely home, and the children. Grey running across the lawn. Little Corey, squatting in her sand pile, laughing up at her mother through the tangle of her yellow hair. Connie's near memory could touch those joys and use them to push Scottie out of her mind.

John loved the children, too, and was a good father to them. He was a playmate for his small children, and a teacher as well. How to throw a ball and catch it, how to tunnel under wet sand and find Corey's toes, how Grey could learn to tie the strings of his diminutive red sneakers. He could on occasion help them to accept their small responsibilities and grow to larger ones.

When the turning points of their lives would come, he would provide a steady, guiding hand for his children to grasp.

Scottie would have done none of those things. Seized by an icy shiver, Connie did thank God that she had had no child by Scottie! She put her hand softly upon John's warm, strong arm, needing to be reassured and comforted. She could forget the past in the reality of her happy present. She wished all women could know that happiness.

She wondered if she might talk to Irene, try to show her what she was risking. Not knowing the man, Connie would put Cliff Adams in the Scottie Stringer class—the importunate, the ruthless, the corrupt. If she could tell Irene how hurt she had been, and how lucky she was now to have a man like John—like Birch—Buell.

Could she do that?

Perhaps she could have done it, but she did not. She had never been close to Irene; the other woman had resented Connie's unwillingness to share her home with Birch and his wife. Now it would have been most difficult to assume the intimacy such a talk would need.

So Connie said nothing. Things seemed to continue in their usual unstable way in the house down the hill. She herself was busy in her home; for days John kept long hours catching up with his medical obligations. It was at the end of the next week before they went anywhere socially.

This occasion was a wedding reception at the country club on Saturday evening. John had not been able to make the wedding itself, and Connie waited for him so that they could go to the club together. She was looking as he best liked to see her—pretty, young. Her dress was of a thin, rosy pink material, floating away from her slim body. Her black curls were tied up and away from her face with dark blue ribbons that fell to her shoulders.

"You look like a bride yourself," John told her when she came out to his car.

"You must care for older women," she teased him saucily.

"Older than what? Corey?"

Connie laughed. "She and Grey decided that they could just as well go with us today. It seems Grey *likes* the club."

"On the Fourth of July," agreed Grey's father. "Did you

tell him there would be no fireworks?"

"No. I told him there would be avocado salad. As you know, he hates avocado. He urged me not to eat any."

The party was in gay swing when they arrived; the receiving line was beginning to disintegrate, but Connie did get to see the bride, and the bridesmaids' dresses. John said he was starved and hoped there would be more than champagne. . . .

Of course there was more, and a lot of their friends were available, too, standing about, or seated at the small, flower-decked tables on the wide veranda.

John always said he hated "bashes," but he always had a fine time at them. He did that day, and so did Connie. She was popular among the social set of the big city and its suburbs. Had she cared to take a more active part in their life, she would have been very welcome. As things were, a fuss was made over their advent at this affair, and a dozen people tried to draw them into their particular circle of discussion and fun.

Once Connie found herself separated from John, but soon sought to rejoin him. She waited while he continued his interchange with the rector who had performed the marriage and a prominent attorney. The men were talking about the ethics of heart transplants, of all things! At a wedding.

Connie put her hand lightly on John's arm as a signal that, when he was free, she had something to say to him. Meanwhile she stood patiently, half listening to what was being said, shaking her head when asked if she had anything to say on the subject. The satin ribbons and her dark curls swung enchantingly against her shoulders. And she watched Beeze.

He was being—"Amazing," she told John when he was free to listen to her. "Just *look* at him!"

John did look, standing even taller to see across the heads and backs of a hundred people. "He's making out with the Riddle twins," he told his wife. "So what's the excitement?"

"He's doing more than making out," said Connie. "*Look* at him."

"I am looking."

"Mhmmmn," said Connie. "Keep watching him. We'll get closer."

"If we can."

"Keep watching," said Connie again.

John did keep watching, as best he could. The Riddle twins were young girls—making their debuts that summer, he thought—pretty girls—one of them was very pretty. They both had nice figures, dark hair—

"Hmmmn," said John Buell.

"You see what I mean?" asked Connie. "He won't be diverted."

"No-o."

Beeze was always popular. Beeze was always "making out" with some young woman, and then another, and another. But this evening he was restricting his attention to the Riddle twins; he leaned toward them, and talked to them. He kept them supplied with champagne and food from passing trays. He only smiled vaguely at those who came up and would have distracted his attention, or would, even, have joined that little group against the topiary tree in the far corner.

"It is rather amazing," said John finally. "He looks absorbed."

"I think he is absorbed. And he doesn't want any other man—"

John laughed. "Sent that guy on his way, didn't he?" he asked, delighted. "I wonder what line he is playing . . . ?"

He and Connie edged around the circle of the room, speaking to people, not too obviously watching Beeze, but watching him all the time.

"They're lovely girls," said Connie, her eyes shining with the excitement of this new development.

The Riddle twins were lovely. Eighteen or so, wearing white linen that evening, a coral flower in their dark hair, one over one right ear, the other over the left. Carrie Lee and Sophia, their names were.

Connie had no trouble discovering their names, because now others were watching Beeze and talking about him. His friends decided that Beeze Buell may have finally been snared. He was, they agreed, actually courting those girls—

"But that's ridiculous," said Connie to John.

"I'm not so sure," her husband demurred. "I believe they are right. Beeze does seem intrigued."

"You thought he was using a new line."

"At first, yes, I did. But he seems entirely too absorbed, and he's keeping it up—"

"Do you think he's fallen in love with *two* girls?"

"You're jealous," teased John. He always claimed that Connie was more fond of Beeze than she would confess.

"I'd be more than jealous," she retorted now, "if I thought he was serious about two girls!"

"I don't think we have to worry about his committing bigamy," John told her. "Look. Can't we go home?"

"Of course." But Connie kept looking back at the threesome in the corner.

"Which girl do you suppose he'll settle on?" John asked, still teasing her.

"I don't know," she said. "The pretty one, I suppose."

"Mmmm, I don't know," John argued. "The pretty one—I think that's Carrie Lee—probably bolsters his ego. Though I will say that scarcely needs doing for our Beeze."

Connie laughed. Beeze was a charming and spoiled young man.

At the door, John paused to look back along the wall at his brother. Now Beeze had both girls by the arm and was leading them away from the topiary tree. At that minute he was talking very earnestly to the girl on his right.

"Somehow I believe he likes the plain one better," said John. "Isn't there a proverb or a quotation about falling in love with a pretty girl, but being wise and marrying her sister?"

"Well, at least now it is a saying," said Connie. "But I don't think you should repeat it to Beeze."

"He'd appreciate it."

"He probably would. And take it as some sort of advice."

John said nothing; he went out to ask for his car. When Connie joined him on the steps, she was still thinking about Beeze. "I think you—we—should keep out of this matter," she told her husband.

"What matter?" He helped her into the car, tipped the boy, and went around to his own seat.

"I think you shouldn't offer Beeze any advice on this romance, if it is one," Connie told him.

"Who, me?" asked Dr. Buell innocently.

She laughed. "Yes, you," she told him. "Let's try keeping out, shall we?"

"Sure will," agreed John cheerfully. "Did you have any avocado at the party?"

"No, but don't tell Grey."

As they drove into their own grounds, they immediately sensed that something was wrong—at least that a crisis had arisen. Grey came running across the circle of lawn, Corey stumbling behind him; she was endeavoring to carry one of the cats. Cleve stood on the stoop, obviously waiting for them.

John touched Connie's knee reassuringly and got out of the car. "I'll rescue Sin," she told him.

Grey was already screaming at them, a jumble of words and phrases.

"The pump's broken down," John said loudly, clearly, so that Connie could hear.

"Don't go down there in your silk suit," she called to him, stooping over the baby. By then the Siamese was ready to scratch his way to safety.

She heard John sending Grey to her. "Tell your mother what happened."

For nearly a hundred years, the Buell estate had gotten its water from two deep wells. That water was as clear as crystal, as hard as iron, and it required pumping. The water itself never failed them, but the pump had a way of doing so. That, or the lines into the house could freeze—break—

While Grey babbled excitedly to her, Connie watched John talk to Cleve, then dash into the house to change his clothes; she would follow suit. If, as Grey indicated, there was water in the lower level rooms—the laundry, the children's playroom, the guest suite down there— Sometimes the pumps failed, and no water was to be had. Today they seemed to be getting too much.

She listened to Grey, she walked toward the front door—slowly, holding Corey's hand. John came out of the house in blue denims, a pull-on shirt, and sneakers.

"We should connect to the county lines," he fumed. "Get

our water from the river like everyone else."

"River" to Grey meant the small, swift stream at the foot of their hill. "We can carry it in a bucket," the child told his father.

John held out his hand. "Come on, son," he said. "Let's go see what can be done."

"Did you call the pump man?" Connie asked her husband.

"Cleve had done that. But it's Saturday evening, remember."

"Oh, but—"

"He'll come, but fishing or his pinochle game could take precedence. Meanwhile Grey and I will put our fingers in the dike."

And meanwhile Connie must console small Corey, who was never ready to recognize her smallness.

"The men will fix things," Connie told the child. "You can help me change my dress and wrap up my ribbons."

Corey would ruin the blue ribbons, but that was a small price.

"Daddy fix?" asked the baby, satisfied with the bribe.

"Oh, of course," said Connie. "There never was a problem that Daddy couldn't fix."

4

By midnight the pump was repaired. On Sunday, Connie and John went to church, telling each other that Grey was getting old enough to attend services. Several friends played croquet with them that afternoon. On Tuesday, with Madie to help, Connie took the children into the city for summer clothes. Their sizes changed so rapidly that she thought it best to have them available for try-ons.

This was wearying for everyone. It took Wednesday for them all to recuperate.

It was Thursday evening when John said that he must stay in the city. There was a staff meeting, or something of the sort. He told Connie, and she knew where he could be reached, but the details did not matter. John was a successful surgeon, and a busy one. She would rather have him at home, but she lost no time or energy disliking the times when he could not be there.

She ate dinner with the children, then played croquet with them for a half hour, a game all in itself, of course. Madie suggested that she would be tired.

"I am," Connie admitted, "but I'd like to put them to bed, if you don't mind."

The young nursemaid looked at her mistress in amazement. "Why should I mind?" she asked.

"Well, I've heard that mothers spoil their children, and if you'd have to cope with the results . . ."

"Yes, ma'am," said Madie. "I ain't worryin' about havin' to *cope*. I know you like to do what you can for the kids."

"Like explaining to Grey why there is no Sunday school in the summertime?" asked Connie, smiling.

Madie shrugged. "You can try," she said.

Getting the children to bed was a lengthy process. Grey no longer wanted to share his bath with his sister, nor even the bedtime story. He was privileged to stay up a half hour later. He made the most of this advantage; he found diversions; he went out on the deck and reported that Cleve and Emma were going home. They lived in what used to be the gatehouse of the estate. He thought up a dozen reasons why he should not come and get his bath.

Could he first have just a little cup of milk? He held his small hands an inch apart to indicate the size of the cup. He was working on Connie, and she knew it. But, yes, he could have the milk.

The kitchen in that house was a wonderful place. Connie, happily, would have liked to do the work there, cooking, cleaning, serving. She agreed with John's decision that they must have Emma and Cleve, but still the shining cabinets and countertops, the gleam of stainless steel, fascinated her.

She gave Grey his small glass of milk. Then, he assured her, they must wash the glass. "We could do the dishwasher?"

Connie shook her head and held out her hand for the glass. "We'll rinse it," she said, holding it under the faucet. "We'll stand it upside down for Emma to put in the dishwasher tomorrow. And then—"

"Why aren't you in bed, young man?" asked a voice behind them. Connie and the little boy both whirled. Grey ran, shrieking, into Birch's arms. "Look who's here!" cried the child. "Mommy, look who's here!"

Connie laughed. "Hello, Birch. I'm trying to get Grey to bed."

"Hmmmn," said Birch.

"He's a great tactician, John says."

"Where is John?"

"He had a meeting. Did you want . . . ?"

"Company. Can I help you with this young scamp?"

"What's a scamp, Uncle Birch?" asked the child, dancing up and down. "What's a *scamp?*"

"A scamp," said Birch, seizing the child, tucking him under his arm, and going toward the bathroom, "is a young man four years old who is about to get scrubbed and thrown into bed."

"Thrown?" asked Grey, his eyes wide as his head came through his pulled-off t-shirt.

"Thrown!"

This so intrigued Grey that the bath went quickly and smoothly. Birch lounged against the door frame and watched Connie. "I'll do the throwing," he offered when Grey was pink and damp and, even, getting a bit sleepy.

The throwing was accomplished, and Grey demanded that Uncle Birch read to him.

"Serves you right," Connie told her brother-in-law. "I'll go put on a dry blouse."

"But, see here—"

"Time you learned," said Connie, already halfway down

the passage. "The rule is one story, read once."

She was back in time to kiss Grey and hear him tell Birch that Babar was pronounced *Barbar*.

Birch was breathing a little faster when he followed Connie to the living room. "I can see it takes training," he said.

"It does. Do you wish you had children, Birch?"

"Of course I do. But Irene says she'd make a lousy mother, and I'm afraid I agree with her."

So did Connie. "Sit down, won't you?" she asked. "There will be at least two drinks of water to get."

"What did you do with Corey?"

"Oh, she protests, but usually she falls asleep in the tub. In another two years she'll be doing the way Grey does now."

"And he'll have thought up other stunts."

"Probably."

Birch sat down for five minutes. For another five he wandered about the room. He talked of inconsequential things—some sort of mold that had appeared on the evergreens, the move of close friends to California—

"I'd better be getting back home," he said then. At the sliding door to the deck, he turned. "Look, Connie," he said. "I see you're alone in the house. . . ."

"Yes. I told Madie she could have the evening."

"Well, yes, but out here in the country— I didn't have a bit of trouble getting in. Don't you think you should lock up?"

"Oh, Birch—"

"Cleve's at the gatehouse. I'm down the hill. But my point is, you and the kids are up here alone. Lock the door after me, won't you?"

"I'm not afraid. . . ."

"Maybe you should be. If I can get in without your hearing me, some thug could too."

"Oh, Birch. . . ."

"There are thugs about. Down at the river—the main road is only a quarter mile away."

Connie got up and came toward him. "All right," she agreed. "I'll lock the door."

"How about downstairs?"

"Cleve locks that when he leaves. The garage door is electric and kept closed."

"All right then. I just don't want you to be frightened, let alone hurt. Maybe I should check the other doors here on the deck—"

"I'll do it," she promised. There were other doors—from her bedroom, the dining room, and the hallway between the children's rooms.

Birch left and before Connie sat down again, she did check on the sliding doors. She felt sure Cleve would have locked the first floor. Anyway, they never had had any trouble. The chow raised a racket if strangers came on the grounds. Of course, he barked at imaginary things, too. . . .

Connie went back to the living room and curled up in the big square chair under the lamp. She would rather have John at home, but since he needed to be away so often, she knew how to amuse herself. There were records, the TV—two new books on the table, a stack of magazines. She picked up the first of these and turned the pages. Once the dog, Yang, barked fiercely, and Connie lifted her head. She frowned a little. She wished Birch had kept still; she didn't want to be afraid.

She got up and drew the gold silk curtains partway across the wide windows. She went in to check on the children, and came back through the kitchen, where she picked up an apple.

Back in the living room, bright with its yellow and orange

white-flowered chairs and couch, its white-shaded lamps, its books and pottery and pictures, Connie put Beethoven's "Eighth" on the player. She liked that symphony, and played it often. Perhaps because whoever had written the material for the album cover had said the music was not well known, that it was not played frequently.

Even as she sat listening, Connie recognized this perversity in herself. She was not a rebellious person, but she often found herself ready to try the less popular colors, the foods. . . . Tonight she had exchanged her crisp white blouse for a bulky, cotton-knit sweater of pale green. This, worn with her white denim skirt, was both pretty and comfortable, but another woman would not have chosen it. She had tied a dark blue ribbon about her hair. She cuddled down into her chair, ate the apple, listened to the music, and let her thoughts wander.

Birch wanted children—John surely would not be very late—there was a little rash on one of Corey's forearms—she would try to get some veal when she marketed this week—

It was a small noise. On another night she would not have noticed it, but Birch had put her on the alert, and she lifted her head. She listened closely, but she heard nothing further. She decided that there had been no noise. She reached for one of the new books, and her outstretched hand hung suspended. She *was* hearing something! A faint click, a whisper of movement—and a shadow was moving across the wall, a shadow cast by the light at the door—a shadow too big to be one of the cats, or a child coming from the bedroom. . . .

Watching the shadow, slowly Connie put her feet to the floor; she rose out of her chair and whirled, all in one swift move.

Her hand went to her mouth. Beyond the stones of the fireplace—he must have come in through the front door—he must have come across their lawn, or along their driveway—in through the double front doors, across the slate floor of the foyer—Connie had heard the whisper of his canvas shoe against the stone— This man . . . this man . . .

Connie stood frozen, her fingertips icy; she was shaking—inside at least. She could hear again Birch's warning. "Check the doors—out here in the country—"

She had not checked the front door. The family used it seldom. It was kept locked—most of the time. Very often, Connie, finding it locked, had had to go around to the terrace, to the steps up to the deck, and then into the house.

But tonight, this man—

Her throat and mouth were dry. And her eyes stared roundly at this man. He wore a t-shirt, not fresh or clean, and brown slacks.

She gasped sharply. Afraid for herself, for— The *children!* Her eyes darted away from the intruder. If he would move to hurt those children . . .

A shudder seized her, and she put her hand back to steady herself against the chair. She bit her lip to regain some control, and looked again at the man. Tall, dark—curly hair, his face weathered—he was smiling a little, and, after what had seemed minutes and minutes of just standing there looking at her, he began to move toward her. One foot, then the other—

Involuntarily, not really knowing what she did, still held in that suffocation of fear, Connie fell back, away from him. Her hand brushed the fireplace stone. Beyond, it would find the long-handled poker, the long, forklike—She gulped, trying to find reality somewhere. She could not believe that this was happening to her!

She had been a nurse. A time or two she had been in danger

from an actual physical threat. But not like this! Those times she had known a clear-cut fear, an anger—

But tonight she knew terror itself—terror which engulfed her, stifled her—made her limbs helpless and her voice a wad of cotton in her throat. That this should happen—to *her*—to John. To the children!

This was more than physical fear, though that was real enough. The very room stank of danger. She had not thought she would ever be so frightened again.

Because—Scottie was *dead!* He could *not* be standing there in her living room, his clothes rumpled, his skin glistening with perspiration—his eyes—his smile—

Oh, this could not be! Scottie could not come into her home, he could not be walking slowly across the green carpet, past John's pipes on the table—

John!

She felt hot tears sting her eyes. And she would not cry! She would not let this man know. . . .

She put her fingers to her lips and walked away. Reaching one of the straw-seated stools, she stopped and turned. "But—" she croaked. "You're dead!"

"Oh, no." And he laughed. "Not me. I'm not dead."

"But—"

He just stood there, shaking his head and smiling. "No," he said again. "I'm not dead. There was a mix-up. There were four of us in this car smash-up, you see. One man was killed. His name was Bill Scott. You see? Him—Bill Scott—two other guys, and me. William Scott Stringer. The newspapers got us mixed up—your newspaper must have picked up the account, and the mistake. I'm not dead."

He couldn't be—she was staring at him. She could see the gleam of his oily skin. He was very sun-browned. The lamplight caught in his curly black hair, his mouth—

Connie could only stand and gaze unbelieving at this man—who—was—not—dead.

He was watching her, too. And he moved, quickly now, to stand close to her. She could feel his warmth, smell his body. If he touched her, she could not guess what she would do. He was looking down at her, leaning closer—then, to her intense relief—he turned away.

"You always were the prettiest girl I ever knew," he said softly. "So clean, so touch-me-not. The way your hair curled against your neck—"

By such means he had charmed her when she was a high school girl. Now he would make her weep, and beg—and she did not want to do either thing.

He was moving about the room, looking at things, touching things. Connie glanced toward the telephone. If she could pick it up, dial Operator, and scream—before he knew what she meant to do, and would stop her . . .

He would stop her. She knew how his hand would seize her arm, how he would pull her one way and push her another. He had used to do those things—bruising her soft skin, humiliating her spirit.

But the telephone was the only thing she could think of to do. She took a step toward the desk, and another—always watching Scottie.

He was looking at everything, the pictures above the couch, the books on the shelves. He moved toward the windows, and his hand found the cord that would open the draperies. He opened them and closed them again. He nodded, and came across to the fireplace. He picked up the little cup from the low table, looked at its bottom, and set it back. Connie made an audible sound of relief and he grinned at her. His finger flipped the flowers in the pottery jar. He had an approving and almost proprietary air. His hand stroked the cushion of the big flowered couch, as if he judged the texture of the linen, and his toe rubbed the green carpet underfoot in the same way.

"Nice," he said a time or two—as a man would speak when about to take possession. "You're looking well, too, Connie. I like the way you're wearing your hair. You're thinner, and it is becoming. And you really do have a nice home. It shows what money and taste together can do."

He stooped and examined the hearthstone. "Solid slab," he said, marveling. "Must have taken some doing to bring that in." He stood up and dusted his hands together, then moved swiftly.

He was going to touch her. Connie backed away, and she screamed. "Don't touch me!" she cried shrilly. "Don't you dare touch me!"

But he did touch her. Just as she had known he would, as she remembered—one hand reached for her wrist, he pulled her close, his other hand went over her mouth, roughly. His face bent close to her. His eyes were cold and menacing. "I'll touch you," he promised. "I'll do anything I want to you."

She could only shake with horror, with fear. If John would only come—though he might be hurt—

"Don't you know the spot you're in, Connie?" Scottie was asking her. "You must have lied to marry the guy. Dr. John Grey Buell!" His voice rasped and roughened each letter of the name.

"You're in a spot," he said again, releasing her, and so roughly that she fell against the couch; the mark of his hand was red upon her forearm. But fear held her so tightly that she could scarcely breathe or think. This man, his touch, his smell—

". . . better be careful," Scottie was telling her. "What you say, and what you do—"

Because she was afraid she might fall, Connie dropped to the couch and sat there, huddled, terrorized. The "spot" she was in—John, the children—the light caught on the rings on her finger—her marriage, her home—

"The thing for us to do," Scottie was saying, speaking excitedly and rapidly, "is to look at this situation realistically. We've got a good thing going here, if we play our cards right. Rich man, professional man—"

"How did you find me?" Connie asked. She had stopped shaking, and was only angry.

Scottie laughed. "That was easy! I met up with a man who lived—or had lived—in Maryville. Our old home town, remember? Me schoolteacher, you schoolgirl?" He leaned against the desk, one ankle crossed over the other.

"I asked this guy if he knew your folks. And of course he did. Knew the whole set-up. I asked about you. He said you were married to this big-shot doctor, and he remembered the name. Told it to me. I looked it up in the medical registry—only John Grey Buell. Had to be the one—so I made my way here. I knew the minute I saw this set-up that my troubles were over. I'd get my wife back, and a rich wife at that."

"You—"

He waved his hand. "I've got it all thought out," he said. "I've been making plans for a week or more, been watching this place. Watching you. Seen you come and go in your good white car. Saw you go to church on Sunday, prim and proper as you please. Man you got is good-looking, isn't he?

One of those sure-of-himself guys. I've seen you playing with your kids. I guess they're yours. And his. Too young to be mine."

Connie shivered. She hated to think of someone—anyone—watching them. He'd hidden in the shrubbery, she supposed. Or even up in a tree. But for a week? Yes. Evidently he could.

"I've looked the house over," he was saying. "I was careful not to let anyone see me. Bribed your dog with good hamburger. Cased the place early mornings, late at night with the lights on. Made the whole scene. Watched your friends down the hill—"

That would be Birch.

"Even talked to the woman there, a bitchy redhead. When she caught me, I pretended to be interested in the old cellar hole. I didn't give myself away, or hang around where she'd see me and get suspicious. But I kept watching. You've got servants now. How about that? Man in a striped coat, white at night. Plump, middle-aged woman in a white uniform, and a good-looking gal, also in white."

He walked over to the small bar and began to make himself a drink, particular about the brand of gin he chose. Connie could have screamed, to see him touch John's things—her things.

Besides, Scottie did not hold liquor well. She remembered. Two bottles of beer made him ugly.

"You've got clothes, too," he was saying to her. "I've watched you. Not the single dress you had when *we* were married. Had to buy you some stuff straight off, but not like the things you wear nowadays. I got an idea those straight little white linen dresses cost a pretty penny. And your shorts—well, anyway. You look cute, and you have cute children.

Boy looks a lot like you—and I can see you and the doctor are crazy about those kids."

He walked out into the room, sipping his drink, and always watching Connie. "Got a lot of nice things going for you, you and the doctor. I figure if he wants to keep all those things, and even if he doesn't, he'll pay, and pay big. . . ."

This was a nightmare. Connie had dreamed parts of it before—that she might not be free of Scottie, that he might show up—that John and the children were the dream—and would disappear.

Huddled down into her pool of cold terror, Connie sat and listened. She watched this man, this Scottie—

He had changed—a little. He looked seedy—and older. Well, of course he was older. Ten years—twelve—how many? Connie couldn't think. But he still was Scottie—the scar on his hairline, the way he used his hands when he talked, the position of his head—the things he said. . . .

Fearing to move a muscle, Connie slowly turned her wrist to look at her watch. If John came home on this scene, this man and his mood, he would kill Scottie Stringer.

When she told him, or when Scottie made his blackmail demands, John and his brothers—the Buells—would kill him. Not really meaning to speak, Connie said this aloud.

Above the rim of his glass, Scottie's eyes slid her way. "I don't think so," he said.

He came closer to the couch, and she drew into its corner, terror again stifling her. He sat down, smiled at her, and put his hand on her knee. She could feel her flesh crawl away from his touch.

"Now," said Scottie briskly. "We should plan this thing we want to do, and we should plan it right. I'll figure the best way, tell you, and you must do exactly as I tell you, to see to it that you don't bollix our chances."

"*Our* chances?" Her soft lips formed the words.

"Yes," said Scottie. "Of course. Whatever we get out of this, you will share in it. You're my wife." He grinned at her. "Or did you forget that?"

Connie felt the room slip away from her, spinning, blurring. . . .

5

THE RINGING telephone brought her to sharp attention. She heard it ring, she looked at it. It rang again, and again—

"Answer it, will you?" Scottie cried angrily.

She stared at him. "I—can't."

"Of course you can." He moved as if to take her arm. She shrank away from his touch. He saw her do it, and a frown drew his eyebrows together.

"Talk naturally," he said, "and don't say anything wrong. You do, and you'll be sorry."

She was on her feet, she walked slowly. He watched her, guessing at her terror. She hoped the phone would stop ringing, but their friends knew that in their big house it sometimes took a while to reach a phone. There was this one, one beside their bed, one in the kitchen—one downstairs—

Her hand shaking, she had to try twice before she pronounced an audible "Hello."

Scottie was watching her, smiling. He took his glass back to the bar and watched her. He set the glass down, selected a cigarette, lit it—watching her.

It was Irene calling. She chattered. Had Connie been asleep? Her voice sounded funny. What had she been doing? Had Connie seen Birch? Was he up there talking to John?

"John isn't at home," said Connie, her voice rustling the dryness of her fear.

Scottie, a fresh drink in hand, the cigarette hanging from his lips, was walking around again. He went to the bedroom, and into it.

Connie could feel the blood drain from her limbs, leaving them cold and limp. He soon came out again, and she took a deep breath of relief. If he should go near the children, or even toward them, she would call the police!

Could she now tell Irene to call them?

She could, she thought—at a price, of course. But she still had a hope—faint as smoke—that she could get Scottie out of the house, and away—with nobody needing to know he had been there. She could bribe him—her thumb felt of the diamond ring on her finger. She could bribe him, get him away, then tell John. Scottie would not be able to get back and hurt her—or the babies. She—

Irene was talking, and talking. Evidently Scottie could hear the staccato rattle of her voice. She said she wanted to come up and talk to Connie. Could she?

She may have been drinking. She said the same things over and over, and the words slipped and blurred. Should Connie say, yes, to come up? It would be a way to get free of Scottie. Irene's being there would be a risk to his "plan," his scheme. Just then Connie wanted time. . . .

But what if Scottie talked to Irene, told her who he was? He might even enlist her aid. And she would welcome a chance to hurt John. Connie, as well. Irene and Scottie together— Panic swept over Connie, closed her throat and shook her from head to foot. "I'm sorry," she gasped into the telephone. "I have a guest. . . ."

Irene said something, but Connie put the phone down as she still talked. She turned to look at Scottie, her dark-lashed eyes wide with fear. "You have to leave! " she said.

He shook his head and gestured with the glass in his hand. "Aw, no," he said. "I'm not moving until we get a few things settled, so we might as well make ourselves comfortable. And speaking of comfort, is there a bathroom in there through that bedroom?"

While he was in there, she could call the police. . . .

He saw what she had in mind, and he laughed. "You'll go with me," he promised. "I remember how nice-Nelly you were about such things, but you'll go with me."

Connie wanted to scream. She wanted to weep. But—

Now, if ever, she must do the right thing—the best thing. Her first need, of course, was to protect the children, to get Scottie away from them, out of the house if she could—

"There's a bathroom," she said slowly. "But it—it's next to the children's room—" She was not a good liar, so she must make every effort to say this just right. "If they'd hear you—us—and would wake up—"

"Make a row, huh?" asked Scottie. "So—we'll just be quiet, won't we?"

"There's another bathroom downstairs," said Connie, gaining some confidence.

"Aw, that's just the garage and the laundry down there—"

"Oh, no," said Connie. "There's a bathroom. There's a guest suite, really—"

Scottie laughed raucously. "Guest *suite*, is it? Well, now—Maybe I should have been staying there all this week. All right, we'll go down to the guest suite."

Connie held herself rigid and walked to the glass doors. "There's an outside staircase. . . ."

"Yeah, I know. I told you I'd cased the house."

Now she was glad that he had, to this extent. Perhaps, having got him out of the main part of the house— She walked along the deck. "It's down there," she said, pointing. "There's a light switch—"

His hand caught her arm; he pulled her roughly to his side. "Oh, no, you don't, sweetheart," he told her. "You're going right down there with me—all the way—"

Well, this, too, would be handled. "Let me go first, then," she said, her voice sounding thin. Her head was ringing.

Because of the stair width, he agreed to this, but he kept his hand on her arm. Halfway down, it moved to her shoulder, and forward to her breast. Connie thought that this time, surely, she would faint. His touch— She clung to the rail, and set her feet warily.

Her shoe touched the concrete, the stone. Perhaps she could hurry now—but Scottie's hold tightened, he pulled her toward him, he bent his head, and she fought him. She pushed hard against him, and struggled—fiercely.

For a small girl, she was strong—and he still was on the steps.

She thought she had caused him to fall. She thought he had struck his head. She only knew that he had released her, and she ran—anything to get free of him. She pulled her clothing straight and ran, fast, around the drive. She remembered that the lower doors would be locked. But she would go in through the front door, lock it, be sure the children were safe —lock the terrace door—

Because he was making no fuss, because he had not followed her, she turned on the terrace lights and looked down the stairs. Scottie still lay where he had fallen, his limbs outstretched, his head back against a step. Was he hurt? She could call an ambulance—the police. She could say he was a prowler. Of course, when he was able, he would tell who he was, who *she* was—

Well, any way this was played, there was bound to be ugliness. Just now the thing was to keep him out of the house, to protect the children first, and herself second. She leaned over the rail.

He was breathing heavily. From the top of the stairs she could hear him. And he looked strange, his color was ugly. . . . Drunk? Faking a collapse of some sort, to get her to approach him?

She went back into the house and locked the door. Later she knew that, right then, she should have called the police. But instead she descended the inside stairs, meaning to be sure the doors on that level were locked—and this check brought her to the door of the playroom, where only the screen was locked. Scottie still lay on the steps, she could hear the way he was gasping—his hand clutched at his chest. He was calling to her.

"Connie," he gasped. "My heart—"

She stopped with her hand on the glass door. That breathing—stertorous was the term—labored, painful. If Scottie was not faking—he had a heart condition. He could not pass an insurance examination, nor one for hard work—

If he were not faking, Connie could safely go out and look at him. Then she could call the ambulance, send him to the County Hospital—a "man came to my home and collapsed."

Slowly, hating to do it, still frightened of Scottie, still terrified of what this night would mean to her, she slipped through the doors and went the few steps to his side.

She bent over him, now afraid in another way. This man was sick! His skin was ashen and beaded with great drops of moisture; his breathing was even more labored. With the instinct of a trained nurse, she took his wrist between her fingers, counted his pulse. There was the look of death upon him. She dropped his wrist and stepped back. If he should die . . . Her heart jumped—with hope. Wild. Exciting. Oh, it was a terrible thing to hope that a man would die! But *this* man— He would hurt her, and John—and the children. He already had hurt them all, just by being alive. He—

"Help me!" Scottie gasped.

Connie stood clear. "I'll help you," she said. "Do you have medicine?"

"No. Heart—"

"I know. Be still. I'll get help. I'm a nurse myself. Lie still."

"Step—back—"

He was right. The edge of the lowest step must be gouging into his back. She should get him flat on the ground. Was she strong enough? She did not want to touch him, but even though she called an ambulance, first he must be made comfortable—as much comfort as could be given to a man who was showing every symptom of a coronary attack.

She could call Cleve to help her. Not Birch. Birch would need an explanation. But Cleve—she could phone the gatehouse, say, "Something has happened. I need help." He would come right up, and when he came, she could say, "This man came here tonight. He became ill."

"Is he a friend, madame?" Cleve might say.

"I know him. Yes."

But there would be no scandal, and no question, either.

If she could call Cleve—

She stood away from Scottie, watching him, and again,

anew, she felt terror engulf her. Sickeningly. The terror she had known upstairs had been nothing to this fear. For—what if Scottie did die—here on the doorstep of her home?

Her real terror, she knew, was not lest he die. Her fear was that he might live—and it was terror indeed. She held her skirt away from him, and watched him. If he was having a coronary—and he did appear to be—

She heard the car. She saw lights come into the grounds, touch the treetops, slide away. She heard the garage door open and the car come into the garage. . . . Connie gasped and ran into the house, across the playroom—she met John at the foot of the inside stairs.

"Oh, John!" she cried, springing at him. "Oh—John!"

"Hey, hey, hey!" he cried, holding her. "Don't knock me down, sweetheart. I'm glad *you're* glad, but let's take things a little easy, shall we?" He was laughing, and he swung her in a half circle, as he would have swung Grey or Corey, playing with them.

Then he straightened, put her to her feet, and bent to look at her. "Has something happened, Connie?" he asked. His face was entirely concerned.

"Yes." She only glanced at him, then walked across the playroom, kicking some blocks out of her way. The children were supposed to pick up their toys before suppertime. . . . She thought of that through the numbness which now held her. She pushed the door open and stepped out. At once John saw Scottie.

Swiftly he went to him and bent over him, turned back an eyelid, felt of his pulse. He looked over his shoulder at Connie. "Who is he?" he asked.

Connie stood with her hand over her mouth. She could

only shake her head.

John's strong arm lifted Scottie's shoulders and edged him flat on the paving. He smiled reassuringly at Connie. "Poor kid," he said. "He's scared you half to death. Did he come here? Were you alone? Where's Cleve?"

"He—went home—about seven-thirty."

Again John was bent over the fallen man. Scottie did not speak. "Cleve should stay up here until I get home," the doctor said, his tone worried.

"Oh, no!" Connie protested.

John stood up and got out of his suit coat. Connie took it. She was thinking that Cleve really should stay around. Tonight—Scottie would not have come into the house. He had been waiting his chance, when she would be alone. He had watched Madie leave, then Cleve and Emma—

Holding John's coat in her hands, feeling the warmth of his body still on the cloth, breathing the faint, but pleasant, aroma she connected with him—shaving lotion, antiseptic soap, his pipe—Connie began to tremble. And for the first time in the past hour, tears filled her eyes. She gasped. John glanced at her and lost no time telling her to get a hold on herself.

"Go to my car," he said briskly, exactly as he would have spoken to an assisting nurse at the hospital. "Get my bag—and there's a small oxygen unit. It isn't very heavy. Make it quick, will you, Connie? This man—"

He bent again over Scottie. Connie knew he had detected her near-hysteria. And he had used the best means possible to settle her down. She was a nurse, trained to take orders.

She went through the length of the house to the garage; she found the case, and the small tank of oxygen. She brought them back.

"Could I go change into a blouse?" she asked, her voice thin.

John glanced up at her. He was opening his bag, taking out his stethoscope.

"This sweater . . ." she explained. She still was obsessed with the idea of calling the police at her first chance to be free of Scottie. Even with John there, she still wanted to seize this chance.

"Change if you want to," John said, bending over his patient. "Then come help me."

Up in her room, Connie collapsed against the side of the bed. If only she could awake and know this for a nightmare. If only she need not go downstairs again, see Scottie, touch him. Dragging her limbs as if they were heavy weights, she went to the closet, took out a cotton dress, stripped off her sweater, stepped out of the skirt. . . .

"Shouldn't we call an ambulance?" she asked John when she came down the stairs again. He was massaging Scottie's chest. "Rub his legs," he told Connie, the nurse. As a wife she did not feature just then. "Roll up his pants leg, massage—" He showed her how. She bit her lip and obeyed, hating to touch Scottie. The hair grew thickly on his legs. All over his body.

"How'd you say he got here?" John asked her. Then, not waiting for her reply, he rummaged in his bag, talking to himself. He told Connie things to do. He worked himself. A syringe—he didn't ask any more questions. He worked, and expected Connie to help him. She did.

Finally, he asked if she could help carry Scottie in to the couch in the playroom. She did help him. John administered a stimulant and stood back to watch its effect. Connie fetched towels, a sheet—

John talked to himself, and to her, but not as if he meant her to pay much attention. "Ventricular tachycardia . . ." he muttered. "Classic picture of shock . . . Might try quinidine sulfate every three hours—intramuscularly. Adrenalin, maybe . . ."

He did not use the adrenalin, but he put the small mask over his patient's face and administered oxygen, alertly watching the results.

He nodded his head and looked up at Connie. "I think that will do it for a time. Now! Tell me what happened here tonight."

She could not escape. She must tell him.

"Are the children all right?" he asked sharply.

"Oh, yes," said Connie. "Oh, yes!"

John stood up and looked down at her, his face deeply concerned.

"I checked on them," she said quickly. "When I went upstairs to change my dress. You know? I still felt that I should call the police. Even with you here. But the children are all right. I do wish I could find a way to make Grey sleep under his blanket instead of on top of it. Now, Corey, she curls up like a kitten, and doesn't seem to move. . . ."

She was babbling. She could hear herself. And John waited patiently. Listening, but waiting. She could feel panic building within her. If only—

John's firm hand on her shoulder silenced her. "Tell me, sweetheart," he said quietly.

The endearment was too much for her. Tears poured down her cheeks, and John held her against his shoulder. "Though I may drown," he teased, wanting, she knew, to ease her out of her fright and her tension.

Dear John. There for that instant, against his warm strength, Connie made her resolution. If Scottie—if she were *not* married to John—legally—she still was, really. Sin or no, she would continue to be John's wife. She would fight to continue. The children, of course, would need protection, and they would get it. They would get it!

In his embrace, he felt the stiffening of her resolve, and he led her away from the couch, and the man upon it. He found a fresh towel and wiped her face, kissing her when he had finished, as he would have kissed Corey, hurt and frightened. He drew her to a chair and knelt beside her. "Tell me about it," he said deeply.

Connie, there so close to him, safe and warm, did try to talk. Scottie—"this man"—had come in, she said. She had not heard him until he was in the house. She had thought the doors were locked. Yes. She had given Madie the evening off. She frequently did that. She was reading—or listening to music— Oh, she didn't remember.

"Did he threaten you?"

"He was . . ." She lifted her head. "There's Beeze," she said. "What could he want?"

Beeze, indeed, was coming along the terrace, calling out as he approached. "Where is everybody?"

"It isn't late," John told Connie warningly. He meant, he wanted her to get a hold on herself.

He went to the door and called. "We're in here, Beeze."

Beeze ducked his tall head as he came into the room. There was no need, but it was a habit he had. He broke off what he was saying about having to hunt them. "Oh, oh!" he said, leaning forward to look at the man on the couch, at the towels, the— "What have we here?"

John stood between his brother and Connie, to give her another minute in which to seek composure.

"Connie had a prowler," he explained, "and he seems to have had a heart attack. I came in from a staff meeting and found the chap out on the stones. I brought him in here."

"A prowler?" asked Beeze. "Have you called the police?"

"Well—I guess he was a prowler. I don't know what else to call him. He came to the house and collapsed. His business may have been legitimate.'

Beeze went over to the couch and looked down at Scottie, who seemed to be sleeping. Under sedation, he probably was sleeping. Beeze looked around at the open medical bag, the oxygen tank . . . "Who is he?" he asked.

"We don't know. Connie, will you open one of the beds in the guest room? Beeze can help me move our visitor in there."

Connie stared at her husband. "Shouldn't we take him to the hospital?" she asked. Anything, anything, to get Scottie out of her house!

"You open the bed," said John again. "I think we'll keep him here for tonight. This seems to be an easy diagnosis. His collapse has all the appearance of a chronic heart condition. By morning we can tell better what we have. . . . I'll get a consultation then."

Connie walked out of the room. She would prepare the bed. By morning, Scottie might be better—or even dead. She closed her eyes and prayed, swiftly.

"Oh, let him be dead!" she breathed.

The guest room, or suite, on the lower level was an attractive apartment. Its glass doors opened to the terrace and commanded a pleasant view of the valley and the river. There was a sitting room, the bedroom, a tiled bath, and a deep closet. Taking off the brown silk spread, Connie thought, bitterly, that Scottie had never known a room like this. The carpet was soft underfoot, there were lamps and pictures. The sheets were primrose yellow. . . .

She heard the scuffle of the men's feet on the flagstones, and she went to open the door for them and their burden. Scottie was mumbling, but only half conscious. Beeze and John stripped his clothes from him and covered him with the sheet. "That will hold him until morning," said John, kicking the soiled garments out of his way. Connie picked them up and took them to the laundry, loathing their touch and their smell.

When she came back, the men were occupying chairs in the sitting room. John held out his hand to her. She went to him and sat on the chair arm. She was so tired. . . .

"I thought I'd look at the children," she murmured.

"They're all right. You were up there only a half hour ago."

It seemed like hours—and hours. Connie sighed. John got up and put her into the chair, slid a footstool forward. "You're all in," he said solicitously. "You've had a terrible evening."

"Who is this guy, Connie?" asked Beeze, nodding his head toward the bedroom.

Again panic threatened to take over. Connie could feel it sweeping in upon her, like the waves of the sea which she had watched with John only a week or so ago. "Why . . ." she gasped. She gulped and tried again. "He was—just a man. He came here . . . and . . ."

"Walked in on her, up in the living room," John told Beeze. "Didn't he say who he was, Connie?"

"He—well, he was queer. I suppose he felt bad." Connie spoke falteringly.

"And he did frighten you?"

"Oh, yes. Just appearing, the way he did. I thought all the doors were locked."

"Did he threaten you, or harm you?"

"No-o. Not really." Connie held her wrist under the folds of her skirt. "I was startled, of course. He just walked in through the doors— And you read things—"

"You didn't know him?" Beeze persisted.

Connie looked at him, troubled. "I don't understand," she said. "What are you suggesting?"

"Nothing," said Beeze. "Nothing at all, Connie."

John went into the bedroom, and Beeze followed him. From her chair, Connie could see them turn and look at her.

"She looks as if she'd seen a ghost . . ." she heard Beeze say to his brother.

She had, thought Connie. Oh, she had!

But she must get a hold on herself. When the men came back . . .

"He could have been a salesman, or repairman who had been to the house," John explained when he returned. "That's what Beeze had in mind."

Connie shook her head. "No," she said firmly. "I don't know him. He is a stranger."

That was her first lie. Or was it? She had begun lying when Irene called. Now she would find out who Connie's "caller" had been. Now, Connie must go on lying, and being caught, but—

"I don't know what he wanted, really," she said aloud. "He came in—and my chief thought was to get rid of him."

"You were afraid."

"Certainly I was afraid! But mainly I thought of the children, and finding a way to call the police. The man did seem ill—"

"How'd he get outside and down the stairs?" asked John. He told Beeze where and how, on his return home, he had found Scottie.

"He wanted to use the bathroom," said Connie, gasping with relief to be able to tell the truth. "I said he might waken the children, that there was the bath down here. I thought if I could get him outside . . ."

"Did he fall down the stairs?"

"Not really. He collapsed at the foot of them."

Beeze got to his feet again. "I'm going to look around again," he said. "Perhaps he had a car. . . ."

He went outside and along the terrace. Connie said something about looking at the children, and went up the inside stairs, John following her. He checked on the doors there—and came back from the front one with Beeze.

"Those kids would sleep through thunder," said Connie, laughing shakily. She went over to the bar to clean things up. Scottie had left the place in a mess—ice melted on the counter, bottles unstoppered, the glasses he had used. . . .

Beeze was at her shoulder. She picked up the two glasses and held them so John could see. "When he seemed ill," she said, "I tried a drink. . . ."

"And joined him in a Bitter Lemon," laughed Beeze. "I know."

She smiled, which was another way of continuing the lies she was telling. The drinks had been Scottie's idea. He had mixed a second one, in a second glass. At that stage of her terror, Bitter Lemon, or anything else, would have choked Connie. She . . .

"Offering liquor to a tramp was not such a good idea, sweetheart," John told her, his tone kind. He was believing her. Beeze was not.

"That's right," Beeze agreed. "We can all be glad that what was due to happen, did not happen to you, Connie."

But it did! thought Connie. It did!

They went downstairs again; John asked Connie what she had done with the man's clothes. He followed her to the laundry and examined them. They told nothing. Slacks, t-shirt, tennis shoes, undershorts and thirty-five cents in the pocket of the slacks.

"There's no car on the grounds up here," Beeze said. "May be one down on the river road. I figure he came up from the river. He'd have his identification, probably in a wallet, in a coat or something he'd left down there."

"There are no car keys," John pointed out.

Beeze shrugged.

John went in to look at his patient; he used his stethoscope again. Scottie made no response. "We won't try to question him tonight," said the doctor. "We'll let him rest."

"He can't stay here, John!" Connie protested.

"He shouldn't be moved, my dear. And there's no need to move him. This is a big house. I'll get a nurse. . . ."

He was watching her keenly. Had this man threatened her, frightened her, beyond what she was telling? Beeze was watching her, too. She was not telling the whole story.

"Well—" She sighed. "Of course you can't move him," she agreed. "And I'll nurse him tonight."

"You can't do that!" Beeze protested.

"Why can't I?" Connie challenged him. "I'm a nurse, remember."

"I remember. But it seems to me that you are afraid of this man, and—"

Connie felt her cheeks go hot. "Because he startled me, entering my house as he did. I'm not afraid of him now." She felt of Scottie's pulse to demonstrate. "I should keep some sort of record," she said, going over to the desk for paper and a pencil.

Not afraid? She was terrified, and more so by the minute. Because now her stunned mind was beginning to look forward to what would come, to what would happen, tomorrow, and the next day. If Scottie lived, he would talk. If he talked to John, he would reveal that Connie had lied to him, that she could lie. John might believe that she had thought this husband dead, but she had never told him of this husband, and—

If Scottie lived, and talked, others would know. And others, and others . . .

In a pretense of keeping busy, she brough a washcloth and towel from the bathroom and gently sponged Scottie's face, his chest, his arms. Once his eyes half opened, and cold swept over her, chilled her.

There could be, and would be, a scandal. Though that, really, would be the least of it. Connie knew that she was a bigamist and not John's wife. Of course she was terrified. She had thought he was hers. And now, in a matter of minutes, she knew that she could lose him—had lost him.

Once he knew . . .

For the past hour, John and his brother had been watching her with concern, and, she thought, with some suspicion. They seemed to guess that she was not telling the whole truth. What did they suspect? That Scottie was another man in her life, a Cliff Adams?

Oh, John certainly would not believe that! And especially not this man! This man with his gross face, his soiled and shabby clothes.

Knowing who Scottie was would be worse—for all of

them. The word that she was a bigamist . . . John would be crushed. The scandal, of course, but that they both would lose the life he had known with her, their home, their children, their love. It had been a wonderful life—in its every phase! From croquet court to his professional position in the city, he had proudly shared his every interest with his wife. And now . . .

Of course, what it would do to Connie . . . Tears poured down her cheeks, and she gazed through them at the man on the pillows. Curly hair, flaccid mouth, the scar on his forehead . . . Oh, she *hated* Scottie Stringer! She would do anything, give anything, to have him out of her life!

He would hurt them all. But most particularly . . .

She could not warn John—nor prepare him. And she wept again. Afraid, afraid.

She took her towel and cloth back to the bathroom, and while she was there, Beeze called that he was leaving. "Good night, Connie."

She made a sound of response, and she heard the men's feet out on the terrace stones. John would walk with Beeze to his car, and talk to him.

About her? Probably. Both were concerned over what had happened this evening—and puzzled.

As she, too, was puzzled. Why had John not moved Scottie out? Why hadn't Connie gone on and called the police? Fear was the answer for her, but what reason did John have? Perhaps Beeze was asking him that right now.

He was, in a sense. He was asking John if he thought Connie should be left with the strange man.

"In his condition," said John, "he's harmless."

"You're sure."

"I'm sure."

"Well—if it were my wife, and my house, I'd get the bum out of there."

John did not immediately reply or comment.

"Don't you think," Beeze persisted, "that Connie is unduly upset by all this?"

He tried to see his brother's face in such illumination as came from the lights about the grounds and on the corners of the big house.

"No-o," said John slowly. "Not *unduly*. She is upset, of course. The whole incident startled her. To have this strange man appear inside the house which she had thought protected against such intrusion, and then to have him collapse— She probably thought he would die. He did look pretty bad there for a while. But now—the man is helpless, and her concern is for his health rather than her own safety or the children's."

"Don't tell me that her mother instinct has been aroused," Beeze warned.

John laughed. "I won't. But I do think the nurse's instinct, well trained into Connie, has come to the fore. This makes her able to care for a patient whom she, essentially, dislikes and even fears."

Beeze made a rude sound of disbelief.

"You don't buy that?" John asked, amusement in his tone.

"I don't think anyone would buy it."

They had reached Beeze's car, and John opened the door for his brother. "Come out again, son," he said gravely.

"I'm not sure I shall. It's too blamed exciting out here."

John smiled and stepped back.

"Look . . ." said Beeze.

"Yes?"

"Well—I was going to say, or to ask—" He was embarrassed, and his attempt to change the subject came out an awkward effort at best. "Is something wrong with Birch and Irene?" He blurted the question.

"Why do you ask?" John spoke as calmly as if the inquiry had come in the middle of a normal, gossipy evening.

"Well," said Beeze, "I stopped in there earlier this evening —before I came up the hill, I mean—and things seemed rather strange."

"Strange, as in my house?"

"No. You stage your own sort of circus. But down there— well, it was indefinite. Birch offered me a drink. Irene sat on the couch and looked handsome. But there was something in the air. Tension, strain . . ."

"Mhmmmn," said John.

"This Adams chap . . . D'you think . . . ?"

"He's around," said John. "And it does seem evident that Irene should have married a man like him rather than our eminent brother."

"Birch is all right."

"Birch is very much all right. But he is not the gay buckaroo type that Adams appears to be. And lately, since Adams seems to be around a lot of the time, Irene probably makes comparisons. She watches the two men and probably comes up with the same conclusion I have. That she married the wrong man."

"I don't think she did."

"What you think doesn't feature, I'm afraid. Not with Irene, nor with Birch."

"He is doing well in his profession, he—"

"But he isn't the swish-pilot type, and Birch is the first to know that he isn't. It bothers the old hoss, too. Besides, Irene is two-timing him, and he probably knows that. Guesses it, at least."

"I'd think he'd be sure of it."

"A man like Birch wants to believe in his wife."

"Well, I guess I'd want to do that, too."

John nodded and stood thoughtful. "Irene knew Adams before she married Birch," he reminded his brother.

"I'd heard that she did."

"My advice to Birch has been to kick her out, divorce her."

Beeze laughed, surprised at John's ferocity. "Did you accomplish anything?" he asked.

"Not that I know. But if he discussed it at all with Irene, he must have shown that he was aware of what was going on."

"She should listen to him and get out."

"She married him, I think, because Birch was more of a sure thing than Adams."

"Then she should beg for a second try. And Birch would give her another chance, on a promise to clean things up."

"Yes, he would. And maybe she did just that."

"Maybe," said Beeze dubiously. Then he looked thoughtful. "Maybe," he said again, and more certainly. "She didn't give me the eye tonight."

"Has she been doing that?" asked John, amused.

"Well, sure she has. Doesn't she, with you?"

"I'm evidently not her type."

"Or you're immune to her eyes," said Beeze, starting the car.

John shrugged and stepped back. He watched the glowing taillights sweep down the drive. Then, shaking his head, he went back to the house.

6

DURING THE fifteen minutes that John was away from the guest suite, Connie had been busy. She had tidied the room, and the bed; her patient's chin now rested on a crisply turned-back sheet. She had reduced the light in that room to a single small lamp on the desk. Bathroom, sitting room—there was no trace of the disarray and confusion which had earlier disrupted things.

She had brushed her own hair, and her face was serene, all traces of tears washed away. With a skill all her own, she had established the atmosphere of a competent nurse in charge of a sickroom.

John smiled at her. "I'm going to telephone the service for a nurse," he told his wife.

"Oh, no, John . . ."

"Yes, I think I should. I think, really, I should have had an ambulance out here two hours ago."

Connie turned to look at the clock. He was right. It had been two hours. "It is late," she admitted. "And you should be in bed. It would take a nurse a couple of hours to be located and to get out here. I'll sit with him tonight."

This she had determined. She was afraid of what Scottie might say, coming out of sedation; she wanted no other person with him until he would be able to recognize a slice of buttered bread for what it was. This idea had become fixed in her mind. The whole thing was a nightmare, but this one purpose came in clear and strong. She must, at all costs, keep Scottie quiet until his own devious wishes would be again clear to him. Then—

"I'll sit with him," she said firmly. "And I'll get some rest. You are to go up to bed. Madie should be back by eleven. I can't think this man will be sick long, and if he is, he can go to the hospital. But for a day or two, I can manage. The servants will take care of the children, and the house. . . ."

John did not like the prospect. His wife . . .

Connie went to him and put her hands on his shoulders. "You married a nurse, remember?" she said, looking up into his face.

He kissed her. "I remember. But I remember, too, how this man frightened you."

"That was shock. And I'm over it. Now, please do what I ask, darling? Go to bed and get your rest. Tomorrow we can decide what to do next."

"You're not afraid?"

She glanced through to the bedroom and to the sleeping man. "No," she said. "But if you like, we can switch on the intercom."

He consented to that and reluctantly agreed to go up to his own bed. Yes, and sleep.

But even as he set foot on the stairs, John turned again to ask her if she would be all right. "I can sleep down here on the second bed."

She smiled and shook her head. "I'll be fine," she said.

She meant him to believe her, and he did, to a point. He would not get his proper rest, she felt sure. But she was sincere in wanting him to go upstairs, to let her be alone with Scottie and her problem. He would not talk any more that night, but she could sit in the midst of her personal nightmare and spend the hours hunting for ways and means. . . .

This *was* a nightmare. No doubt of that. One which had begun the day she first saw Scottie Stringer. And during this sleepless night she could live again every minute of what had happened to her because of this man. The happenings of her final high school year, ending with the excited peak of their elopment, the shock and the fear of her short marriage, the shame, the actual pain, the real hurt of that time. The desolate waste of the months when she had struggled to come back, the cleansing relief of knowing that she was free of Scottie, the sober pride in building her life anew, the real joy and pride, of knowing John, marrying him, loving him . . . building a life with him, their family, and home. . . .

Only, now, to have it all . . . Oh, dear God, it was a nightmare!

And, as in all nightmares, Connie went over it again and again. She wrapped herself in a blanket and sat in the armchair, her feet on a low stool. Twice during the night, John came down to check on things, and he always found her so, their patient still slumbering. He said a few things in a whisper to Connie; she replied, urging him to get some sleep. Each time he promised that he would, and each time Connie would settle down to think, to go again over the treadmill of what had happened, what would happen.

She still could not face, nor accept without panic, Scottie's physical presence here in her home. Her house with its enormous garret, its thirty-five-foot living room, its— Oh, the whole thing was unbelievable. This was *her* house. She had put John's own brothers out of it to make it hers, a symbol of her marriage and her life. This house, and each thing in it, had become a mark of her goal in life—a goal of safety, honor . .

Once, having reached this point on her treadmill nightmare, Connie stepped free of the blanket and went out on the terrace; from there, she stepped down to the lawn and walked away from the house enough to look up at it, to look at it from one end to the other, to see it all, as one looks at a familiar passage in a book, or at a picture one knows well, to be sure that each detail is there, as she knew it was there, but still—

The house stood there, seeming strong and firm. The terrace stones, the balcony, the roof and its great stone chimney. It seemed as always, but Connie knew that it was not the same. Because tonight a bomb had been placed under the cornerstone of this house, and even now it was ticking away the moments to its destruction.

In that terrible half hour before his attack, Scottie had said enough, and plainly, to show that he had come here to make trouble. "We have a nice thing going for us," he had said to her.

And now he really could make trouble; he would.

Slowly Connie went back into the house. She should have fought Scottie from the first. No matter what physical harm he would have done her, anything—*anything*—would have been better than this! She should have got the police there, and when John came home, she should have told him—and got the police.

But, now, what should she do?

She sat in the deep chair, wrapped in the soft gold blanket, and she stared at the helpless man who could ruin her life.

He was sleeping now, under sedation. In a few hours he would waken, and talk, and—

What was going to happen?

If Scottie was alive, Connie was still married to him. So she would have to leave John Buell's home and find herself a place to live, and a job, get a divorce. She would not go with Scottie! At no cost would she do that!

Her children . . . ? Poor, innocent things. There were ugly words for children in the position where she had put her darlings. Of course John would support them, and care for them—but they would miss their mother, whom they loved. And she would miss them. . . .

Oh, she would miss them! But she could not compromise them, nor John, further. Her escape from them must be as quick, and complete, as her escape from Scottie.

Would John's brothers, and Irene, move back into her house? If Irene were a different person, Connie could find some thin consolation in believing that Irene would take care of her home and her children. As things were—

The Buells would all be shocked and disgusted. They would not relish the gossip which would surely attend these revelations. They would wish, bitterly, that John had never married her, that they never had known her. Beeze's recent interest in the Riddle twins would go up in smoke. People would laugh at the Buells, and talk. . . .

And John. Dear John. He would have to go on, still the same fine surgeon. But patients, colleagues, friends, would know what had happened. And if he loved Connie, as she knew he did—she must know that, or go entirely crazy—he would grieve for the wife he had lost. He would offer to help her, he would be kind—and come to hate her, too, no doubt.

7

INCREDIBLY, the long night did pass. Dawn came with a cool little breeze and a cloudless sky. Scottie was becoming restless, and when John came downstairs, he administered another sedative. "He's coming along," he told Connie. "How about you?"

She smiled wanly.

"You're to go upstairs," he said, "take a warm bath, and get into bed."

"Oh, John . . ."

"I'll speak to Emma. She can keep an eye on things here. I'm not operating until afternoon. I think I'll get a heart man to come out here and tell us what we have. . . ."

"But Emma has to fix breakfast."

"Madie can care for the kids. I'll fix my own breakfast, and yours. Come along, now."

Connie gave in, because she had no choice. Scottie was again dead to the world. She heard John talking to Emma, heard that good woman's tone of shock, surprise, and agreement to help out all she could. "Poor Mrs. Buell," she said.

"To have a man come to the house, and collapse—"

"It won't be for long," John told her. "We'll move the patient or bring in a nurse. I appreciate this, Emma."

"We shouldn't never have left her alone last night."

"No. That's something we have all learned."

Connie took her bath, spoke to the children and to Madie. Sensing a disruption in their small, ordered world, the children were being naughty. Why couldn't they go into Mommy's room? they asked. Why couldn't they go downstairs? Why did Madie cook breakfast? Why was Mommy tired? Who was sick? She didn't sit up all night with *Grey!*

Connie sighed and closed the bedroom door. Poor dears, they were due to be more upset, and more.

She was drowsy when John brought her a breakfast tray, but she ate something—toast, she thought, and some of the children's hot cocoa. Then she went to sleep, to waken abruptly at ten, to sit up and try to remember—

John could not have attended to many of his own affairs that morning. He had talked to George Bennet, his surgical assistant, and to Miss Danford, his personal o.r. nurse. Both of them had told him what he should have done the night before. Both of them had reminded him that he was not a heart specialist. "I don't know why I had to be told that," he would say later.

At ten o'clock he came back to the house, bringing with him a bright little rabbit of a man, a Dr. Rinke, heart specialist—and a technician with a portable EKG machine.

Their arrival awakened Connie, and she was up, into a dress and white shoes and downstairs by the time the technician, a bustling, efficient woman, had things set up at Scottie's bedside.

John greeted Connie with a patient smile and introduced

the doctor and the technician to her. "My wife was alone when this man came to the house and collapsed," he explained.

He went on to tell what measures he had taken. Connie helped the technician set up her apparatus. Dr. Rinke examined Scottie, then he and John stood aside to let the women work at the bedside.

"If you're going to nurse him," said the technician to Connie, "you'll have to raise this bed. These low jobs are murder."

"Are you going to nurse him, Mrs. Buell?" asked the little heart doctor, striding toward them.

Connie looked to John.

"My wife is a nurse," he said. "An R.N. She stayed with the patient last night, but I suppose we will move him. I recognize this arrangement as temporary."

"Hmmmn," said Dr. Rinke. The technician started her machine, and he suspiciously watched the needle make its tracings. The leads were changed, and the tracing proceeded. The instant it was finished, he ripped the paper out and took it through to the outside light to read. The technician said she would not pack up just yet; sometimes Doctor wanted a second reading.

"So you're a nurse?" she said to Connie, her tone doubtful.

Connie supposed she was looking young that morning. She often did. It was a matter of her round eyes, her curly dark hair. The cotton dress she had grabbed from the rack was of pink and white checked gingham.

"Yes, I'm a nurse," she said quietly. "Registered."

The men came back, and Dr. Rinke bent over the patient. "I don't think you have anything too critical here, Buell," he said, straightening and folding his stethoscope. "How old is your man?"

John said that he didn't know. The man was a stranger; he had come to the house and collapsed almost immediately. "I wasn't home at the time."

"I'd put him down for forty-five, maybe a little older," said Dr. Rinke. "This looks like a somewhat chronic situation. I believe, for a few days, rest and medication will handle things. Later, if you want chest plates . . . But since he's here and seems to be responding to what you have done . . . The hospitals are so damned crowded, and unless we'd need to use extravagant means—which are not indicated—you already have a nurse . . ."

John put his arm around Connie's shoulder. "I have a wife," he said loudly. "But I'll get in a nurse."

Dr. Rinke looked at him thoughtfully, and at Connie. "Yes, of course," he said vaguely. He nodded to his technician. "You can pack up," he said.

"I'd be glad to nurse . . ." murmured Connie.

"No!" said John, louder than before. Connie smiled at Dr. Rinke.

He said a little more about medicine and food. "Keep him quiet in bed for a time," he said, going outside.

Connie assured John that she would take care of things until the nurse arrived; there were a few sickroom supplies needed. . . .

She went back to Scottie's bedside. "I'll take over now, Emma," she told the older woman.

"Dr. Buell . . ."

"I had several hours' sleep. And Dr. Buell is sending a nurse."

"Yes, ma'am."

Connie relented. "You can help me change the bed," she said.

Scottie was moving about a little, restlessly rather than as if in pain. He was only semi-conscious. "Because of the sedatives," Connie reassured Emma.

The bed was too low. . . . "I expect the nurse will want it raised," she said, "or a hospital bed brought in. Though that would scarcely pay. Dr. Rinke thought this would be only a matter of a few days."

Emma went to fetch some white sheets. "There's no use usin' the good guest-room ones," she explained as she departed. "I'll bring down one of the doctor's pajama coats . . ." she added.

"No!" cried Connie sharply. She could not bear to have Scottie . . . "This man is heavier," she said lamely. "I'll buy him something after the nurse comes."

Emma disappeared, and Connie moved restlessly about, waiting for her. She could hear the children out at the sandbox, and she went toward the terrace doors. Below her, down the hill, she caught a flash of white, and movement. . . . She stepped outside.

Yes. Below her, going along what was called the river road, was Irene. Her red hair shone in the sunlight, her white blouse and shorts were dazzling. The man with her— Connie moved forward. Blond hair, the way he wore his clothes—it was Cliff Adams. As she watched, he put his hand on Irene's shoulder, and she turned to him, laughing. He hooked his arm through hers, and they went on, disappearing behind the trees that grew thickly at the river.

Connie waited for a moment, interested, as she would be interested in strangers going gaily, carefree, along the road on a

June morning. Would they stay under the trees? Perhaps there was a boat down there, a place to sit and talk. What did young people do at such times?

That morning, it did not occur to Connie that one of the young people was married to John's brother, and had no right . . .

While she watched, they did not come into sight again, and Connie went back into the house. Scottie was watching for her, in his eyes the same curiosity as she had felt about Irene and Cliff. What would they do next? What would Connie do next?

She went across to the bed. Emma was taking a lot of time to get sheets! Probably she was talking to Cleve about the strange things that were happening in the house. The strange man, and the strange way Mrs. Buell was behaving—*not* wanting to use her husband's pajama coat!

"Scottie?" said Connie softly, bending over him. He met her gaze, then closed his eyes. He did not answer.

"He ain't back to himself," said Emma, behind her.

"His eyes were open. I thought he might be awake."

"Yes, ma'am."

They changed the bed; Emma carried the soiled linens away, saying that she might as well put them through the washer.

Connie told her to go upstairs then, about her regular duties. "I'll sit down here. There isn't anything to do. The nurse will be coming."

"Yes, ma'am. Cleve says he'll help."

"I'll call him if I need him. Thank you, Emma."

Next door, the washer began to hum, and Connie heard Emma going upstairs. Madie was talking to the children.

Connie curled up again in the big chair and gazed at Scottie. Alone again with him, dispassionately she looked at him, hating every inch of him, but now her hatred was calm and cold. She could, she thought in that detached way, murder him. Last night, sitting here, she had prayed, profanely, that he would die—that his heart would fail completely. . . .

It had not. But she could make it seem that it had. She could put a pillow over his face and hold it there; she could give him a second dose of the sedative. . . . No, the pillow would be better. She could do it. Shouldn't she do it?

Everyone would be helped. And she had to do something! She *had* to! Quickly. At once.

She could not let this man waken, tell what he would tell, make his demands on her, and on John—

Suddenly, swept anew with terror, Connie ran upstairs. She counted the money in her purse and looked at the balance in her checkbook. She would put the children in her car and leave with them. She would run away. She—

Slowly, she went downstairs again. She could not leave John—nor take his children from him. There was just one thing to do. Scottie must be handled in a way to remove all danger from them. And now was the time to do it. There was no choice left to her.

She could not talk to John and tell him what really had happened to them all last night. Oh, she could. She could even try to persuade him to help her. And he would. Shocked, disgusted, he would buy off Scottie, and let her leave—

Doing that, the whole thing could be kept quiet—which was most important, for his sake, and the children's.

Connie would be hurt. But she deserved to be hurt. She had married Scottie; she had lied to John when she had married him! She was the one who should pay.

Yes, she would tell John and then go away. John would do what was right for the children. She would get a divorce from Scottie and make her way. . . .

Would John go along with this plan? It seemed to Connie to be the only thing he could do. He would be hurt, she thought, and disappointed in her. He had thought she was being honest with him. Honorably, he might even offer to marry her again. . . .

On the bed, the sick man made some sound, and Connie glanced at him. His face was gaining color. Since she had last seen him, Scottie had put on weight, and his cheeks were round, a little puffy. Glistening.

Would Scottie take the money John would pay him and depart? Depart quietly, and stay quiet afterward? Connie shook her head from side to side. No, he would not. He would not let Connie go her way, for one thing. He was including her in his plans. "We have a good thing going for us," he had said last night.

So—she sighed—he needed to be killed. To die. Only in that way could Connie remove the threat to the children, and to John.

Should Connie do it now? Before John came back, or the nurse arrived? And how would she do it?

She got up, went into the bathroom and looked at the medicines which John had set out there on the counter. The heart stimulant, the sedative—there were three or four packages containing disposable syringes. John had trusted Connie to be careful of those things.

She could use the material at hand . . . and have the nurse come in on a dying man.

She could use the pillow, and no one would know. Except herself—and Scottie.

He was, as Emma said when she came down to check on Mrs. Buell, "coming out of it." He hadn't said anything intelligible, but he was mumbling a word or two. And his eyes were open. They followed Connie wherever she went.

"Can you understand him?" she asked Emma.

"Don't try. Man sick as he is wouldn't make sense. Will you come up and eat lunch with the kids, Mrs. Buell? Cleve says he'll sit with him."

For a brief second, Connie hesitated. Then she nodded. "Of course I'll do that. Thank you for suggesting it, Emma. The nurse should be here any minute now."

"Yes, ma'am. Oh, here's Mr. Beeze."

Connie had not heard his feet on the terrace. She whirled in startled surprise. Why had he come? Why wasn't he downtown in his office?

He came inside and went through to look at Scottie. "Hmmmn," he said.

Connie told him that Dr. Rinke had been there, and what he had decided. "John is sending a nurse."

"That guy never had it so good," said Beeze shortly, jerking his head toward Scottie.

Connie looked at him in surprise. "What do you mean?" she asked. She meant, "How do you know?"

Beeze answered her unspoken question. "I helped undress him last night. His clothes were strictly bum-on-the-road. And look at his hands. You've cleaned him up, but his fingernails are broken. . . ."

"Come outside," said Connie. "I think he's gaining consciousness. He'll hear you."

"He knows it's true. You look tired, Connie."

She brushed her hair back from her face. "I suppose I am tired. I'll take a nap this afternoon. What about you? I mean, why are you here, and not downtown?"

"I had an inspection job to do out this way—and I was lonely. Besides, I always like to talk to you."

And why, Connie asked herself, had he thought it necessary to come to the house again this morning?

"Why should you be lonely?" she asked, feeling vague, and probably sounding that way.

"Oh—I'm not being appreciated."

"Beeze . . ." She was too tired for his sort of gay talk. She was remembering what Emma had said. Scottie wouldn't make any sense.

So, for a time perhaps, Connie could relax. It wouldn't matter what Scottie said to the nurse, or to John, or—

"I need companionship," Beeze was telling her. "Preferably sympathetic."

"And lunch?"

"Well, sure, lunch, but—"

"I have a date to eat lunch with the kids," Connie told him.

"Last time, Corey put spinach in her hair."

"She seldom repeats. Anyway, she's off junior foods. Is something wrong, Beeze?"

"With me? I guess, no. But—did you ever meet the Riddle twins?"

"I think so. Pretty girls."

"Nice girls," Beeze amended, and firmly. "I—well—I've been hanging around there. . . ."

"I'd heard." Eons ago, Connie had heard. When she was John Buell's legal, happy wife, together they had marveled at Beeze. . . .

He was absorbed now in his own affairs. "I arranged things so I could spend this afternoon with them. You may know, John is operating on their grandmother, and I thought I could cheer them up, or something. But it seems they want to do the death watch at the hospital. . . ."

"Beeze!"

"What else is it? When you sit out on those hard chairs and wait?"

"If John is operating . . ."

"She's a pretty old lady, and I guess the situation isn't too promising."

"I'm sorry."

"Sure. I thought I could help. But they'll be at the hospital. That's a close family; they all gather round. Besides, it means a wad of money if John doesn't pull the old lady through."

"He will if it is possible," said Connie, going back into the house.

Beeze followed her. She wished he had not. She took Scottie's pulse, and glanced again at her watch. Why didn't that nurse come?

"What about this guy?" Beeze asked her.

"Only what you know," Connie answered. She knew that Beeze was watching her face. "You were here last night."

"Not when he came and you let him in."

"I did not let him in!" Connie cried sharply. "He—" She broke off and went into the bathroom. Beeze strolled back to the terrace doors. He was troubled, not comfortable at all over what seemed to be going on in his brother's home. Tramp or not, that man in there needed explaining. Last night, Connie had been more than just plain scared. And John had known it. Why else would he have kept the prowler here in his home? Something was going on.

And if Beeze was any judge, what was going on, the presence of that kinky-haired ape in her guest-room bed, meant some kind of trouble for Connie. The girl was hiding something; she was not being her usual frank, ingenuous self.

She was also being clumsy about the concealment. It wouldn't take much to find out—Connie couldn't even keep Christmas secrets. If Beeze would try at all . . .

The lunch table was not the best possible place to begin such an investigation. The children were noisily glad to have their mother with them. Where had she *been?* they asked. Did she know that Corey had eaten a whole piece of bacon for breakfast, without cutting it or chewing it? And there had been a bug in the sandbox!

"Bug!" Corey repeated ecstatically.

Beeze did his best to accommodate his long legs to the low table in the playroom, and his rather sophisticated taste to tomato bisque and chicken sandwiches—with animal crackers and vanilla custard for dessert.

He had no better success talking to Connie. She made the children an excuse to ask him not to speak of the man downstairs.

Though the children knew he was there. Grey had told Beeze elaborately that there was a man hurted downstairs, and he had to stay in bed—not even go to the bathroom!—and did Uncle Beeze know he was going to nursery school? "In a day or two. Corey can't go. She's too little."

"Stay Mommy," said Corey contentedly. Connie's heart turned over. If the baby had a Mommy next fall, or "in a day or two."

"What sort of heart attack did your specialist say your man had?" Beeze asked Connie.

"He didn't spell it out, Beeze. I think he said the condition was chronic. . . ."

"What does that mean, medically?"

"I'm no doctor."

"Oh, come on now."

"Well—Corey, pick up your sandwich; don't pull it to pieces. Well, it means—oh, something like a heart condition left from rheumatic fever, or maybe chronic myocarditis. . . ."

"Which do you think it is?"

"I don't know. Madie, would you please bring a damp cloth? Corey has much more soup on her face than she's swallowed."

Beeze kept trying, feeling as if he were rolling a heavy keg up a steep hill. Was the "guy" sick when he first came to the house last night? he asked. Had he been drinking?

"I don't know," said Connie wearily. Beeze need not have shown up and subjected her to this cross examination. He was ready to pounce on the least thing! And finally, when he came out and asked her, flatly, who the man was, she knew that terror was again ready to seize her.

She stared at her tormentor, put her fingertips to her lips and gasped, "I don't know, Beeze! I don't know!"

"Okay, dear," he said quickly. "Okay."

But he knew that she was afraid, and that she was lying. And the whole situation worried him. If she was lying to John, too . . .

He didn't want to think that little Connie was two-timing John. And she couldn't be! Certainly not with that man downstairs. Granted that the guy was not at his best, out with a heart seizure of some kind—but last night, the man had not been *clean!* His body stank of old perspiration—he—

When Madie came to get the children for their naps and Connie went downstairs, Beeze paced the upper balcony and worried about things in this house—about his brother, and his brother's wife. John was entirely too nice a fellow—

Downstairs, her return acknowledged by a brightening in Scottie's eyes, Connie cared for her patient, knowing what Beeze was thinking. If he only could guess how she hated this man! If he could begin to guess the thoughts of murder which he had interrupted that morning. As for believing that Scottie was some secret passion in her life, she wished, she wished that things could be that simple!

Beeze had wanted to talk to her, and he would talk to her now. Kindly, sorrowfully when he knew, and honestly. But Connie could not talk to Beeze about what Birch, teasingly, called her "hungry past." The brothers had so teased her because they thought she had no such past, one that was remotely "hungry." Birch liked her, and so did Beeze, knowing that she was not one of his society girls—with "wads of money." But if he knew to what depths she had sunk . . .

Oh, no. She could not talk to him about it, nor to anyone. This was her problem, one she would have to solve for herself. No amount of talking would make anyone understand her feeling toward Scottie, or comprehend what he had already done to her life.

She wished—oh, *how* she wished!—that she could talk to Beeze, or to Birch. He might be better, because Birch was a lawyer, and a good one. A good man, different from Beeze, and Connie had never been on quite such friendly terms with him. But she liked Birch. She loved him and Beeze both much, she had always felt, as she would have loved and trusted brothers, had she had them.

But, no, she could not talk to them about this. If she did find a way to rid herself of Scottie, they must not be implicated. If she decided that she had to leave, they must not know of her plans. She had hurt John enough.

The nurse arrived at one-thirty, and Connie was too glad to

see her to complain about the time it had taken her to appear. Mrs. Toomey was a licensed practical nurse, a woman about forty, tall, raw-boned, red-haired. Brisk and efficient.

Dr. Buell, she said, had given her his orders. "He said I was not to trouble you, Mrs. Buell."

Connie smiled faintly. "I am glad to have you here, Mrs. Toomey. But I am quite ready to help you, answer any questions. . . ."

"I understand. He thought the patient would be snapping out of his spell pretty quickly."

"Dr. Rinke said he should stay quiet in bed for a few days. But, yes, the situation is not too serious."

Mrs. Toomey looked Scottie over. She read the notes which Connie had been keeping. "He said you were an R.N. What about clothes? Linens? A place for me to sleep? Dr. Buell said there was a houseman who would help me."

Connie summoned Cleve, and explained about the intercom. Emma, she said, would be helpful about meals. The soiled linens could be put in the laundry room. Emma would supply fresh ones. "I'll go out and get some pajamas for him, and anything else you think you will need. Could you sleep in the sitting room here? Won't you have a relief?"

"As a favor to Dr. Buell, I'll stay on the job twenty-four hours. It's not regular."

No, it was not. Connie expressed her gratitude.

"We can put blocks of some sort under the bed legs," she offered. "To raise it."

"That, or put both mattresses on the one bed."

Yes, that would do it. Connie's pretty guest room would never be the same again. . . .

"A cot would do for me," said Mrs. Toomey. "Or that couch in yonder."

Things were soon in hand. Connie took Beeze with her to do the shopping, and urged him to talk about something other than "that man." And he did. He helped her shop for pajamas, for the sickroom supplies Mrs. Toomey wanted. "How come John rates a nurse like that?" he asked.

"He has a fatal charm."

"Especially with nurses, eh?"

Connie stared at him, then recovered enough to smile a little.

"I'm going to take you home and put *you* down for a nap," Beeze promised. "You're beat."

At home, Connie agreed to stretch out on the chaise on the terrace. Beeze promised to keep the children from bothering her. And she did rest, a little. She saw Beeze talking to Mrs. Toomey—and she asked him to give her a report.

"She tells me our patient says he's a friend of the family," Beeze told her.

Connie lifted her head. Then dropped it again. "He's not lucid," she murmured.

"That's what I thought. Oh, gosh, Connic, guess who's coming!"

Before she could sit up, Connie found out who was coming. It was Irene, coming up the hill, hailing the house from fifty feet away, and coming on. She still wore her white blouse and shorts—but Cliff Adams was not with her.

"I heard someone was sick up here," she announced as she reached talking distance. "It's not you, Connie?"

"Oh, no. Beeze thought I was tired."

"You do look pooped."

"Well, thanks a lot."

Irene sat down. She smiled at Beeze and asked him if he could find anybody a drink.

"We're waiting for John to get home," he said, sitting down.

"Connie . . ." Irene pleaded.

"Of course you may have a drink," said Connie. "But will you go up and fix it yourself? Or ask Cleve? We are a little disrupted around here."

Irene went up the stairs, and her high, clear voice came back to them. She was pumping Emma and Cleve—who wouldn't tell her much.

But enough. "Who *is* this man who came here for his heart attack?" she asked Connie when she returned with her tall, frosted glass. "Was he here when I called you last night? I think you said you had company. . . ."

Had Connie said that? She could not remember.

"I was feeling dreadfully low," Irene explained to Beeze. "Connie is such a clear-thinking person, I wanted to talk to her. But she said she was busy. . . ." Above the rim of her glass, her eyes were round. "If this man was here then, I don't think he was sick. . . ."

Irene stayed for a half hour, and chattered constantly. She had managed, on her trips along the terrace, to peer into the guest room, but Connie knew that the bedroom—and Scottie—were not visible from the door. Her visitor had little luck, too, in getting definite answers from Connie or from Beeze. She was amazed, she kept saying, to know that he had been up here the night before. . . .

No one bothered to straighten her out as to the arrival and presence of the various characters in what she repeatedly called the most amazing thing! And finally she departed, saying that she supposed Birch would want his dinner. "I wish we had Emma and Cleve," she said discontentedly.

For five minutes after she left, neither Connie nor Beeze spoke.

"Should I have asked her to stay for dinner?" Connie murmured then.

"Yes, and taken her on a tour of your hospital facilities."

"Beeze, I try to get along with Irene."

"I've stopped trying, and if there is any change in our relationship, it's been for the better."

"Maybe you should tell Birch that."

Beeze chuckled. "I might try it. Car coming. . . ."

"It sounds like John—" Connie was on her feet. "I should have changed. He's early. . . ." She looked in dismay down at the pink gingham which she had worn all day. Her hair . . .

From the way his embrace tightened about her, the look in his eyes, Connie knew at once that things had gone badly with John that afternoon. Had he been worrying about her? Or had something gone wrong at the hospital?

The Riddle grandmother! Oh, dear . . .

"I'll fix you your drink," she said. "Beeze?"

"Make me one, too. I'll hold the fort here."

John took off his suit coat and hung it on the back of a chair. As Connie went up the stairs, she heard Beeze answering his questions. How was the patient? Had the nurse come? Was the man conscious? Had he told them who he was?

"He said he was a friend of the family."

Connie leaned over the railing in time to see John smile faintly and go down along the terrace to see his patient.

When she returned with her tray and the frosted glasses and pitcher—she had stolen ten minutes to change her dress and run a comb through her hair—John was seated on the terrace, telling Beeze about the Riddle twins' grandmother.

"I'm sorry, darling," she said when she handed him his glass.

"We knew we had only a remote chance. Did you make Beeze a drink as good as this?"

"Almost," she answered, glad that she was able to follow their usual line of small talk, all the time conscious of the undercurrent of their warm love for one another.

John sipped his drink, savoring it. "Where are the kids?"

"Madie's kept them busy all day."

"I'm tired," he confessed. "How is Mrs. Toomey doing?"

"All right, I think. I talked to her when she first came, and offered any help she might need. I haven't seen her since."

"She's a capable workhorse. I looked at our man; he seems to be coming along. I'll go down there again in a minute or two.

Connie put her hand on his arm. "You'll rest for that minute, and a few more. I'm sure the patient is all right."

"In clover," muttered Beeze.

"What's that?" asked John, amused.

"Damnedest things I ever heard," sputtered his brother. "Guy comes here, breaks into the house, gets sick—Does he get treated like the burglar and woman molester he probably is? No, sir! He's put to bed on foam rubber and percale sheets, provided with a special nurse, given high-power medical care. You'll *never* get him out of your house!"

John looked up at Connie and smiled. "Listen to the man."

"You know you should have called the police last night," Beeze told him. "Wait till Birch hears how you've exposed yourself."

"I'll wait," John agreed. "And if I hadn't been so tired today when I finished at the hospital, I would have made arrangements to move the man. Connie told me last night he belonged in a hospital, and, as usual, she was right."

"Don't fret about it now," Connie urged. "You do look exhausted. I don't think you should even talk."

John loosened his tie and lay back in the chair, willing to submit to her efforts to make him comfortable.

She would tell Emma to keep the children upstairs; she planned to give John a chance to rest. He'd had little sleep the night before. . . .

Though, if Beeze had not been there, she would have been tempted to try to talk to John. That talking should be done as soon as possible, certainly before Scottie was able to do much talking of his own. He—John—must be warned about the spot she was in, and he, too. But Beeze was there . . .

And truly she was glad for this short reprieve. To have her husband, John, come home and, though tired, offer her every sign of his love—Oh, she could not lose that! Not and herself survive. It was more than love which Connie had from John Buell. He admired her, and many wives did not have that. If Connie could only hope to keep it. . . .

The love he had for her, that was different. Though it, too, could be in peril. For how could John, or any man, love any woman, once it was proven to him that she was a liar and a cheat?

She could not—oh, she could not—lose what she had with John. With Scottie alive, she might not legally be John's wife, but until he knew different, she was going to keep her husband's love, if she could. Any way she could. Should telling him the truth be that way—

Softly she went into the house and talked to Emma. She thought, she said, Mr. Beeze would not be staying for dinner. A tray must go down to Mrs. Toomey. . . .

"She's spoke about that, ma'am," said Emma.

"Yes, I expect she has. It won't be for long, Emma."

"No, ma'am."

"Ask Madie to keep the children busy; their father needs an hour or so of rest."

"Yes, ma'am."

Connie turned away, then she came back. "We appreciate what you are doing, Emma," she said warmly.

The older woman smiled. "Yes, ma'am."

When Connie went downstairs again, Beeze was on his feet, ready to depart. "I can see I'm not staying for dinner," he said plaintively.

"Shouldn't you go see the Riddles?" Connie asked him coolly.

He nodded. "Yes, I should. You two keep things going here. Get rid of your star boarder. I'll stop and tell Birch you need help."

John stirred."I can tell him that myself, if necessary."

"See that you do it then," said Beeze, walking along the terrace.

Connie went with him, and around to his car. "John is very tired," she offered in apology.

"I can see that. Now, tell me. Why does he keep that man here?"

She summoned strength. "It is John's way to care for the sick," she said. "Even to offer his home if necessary. And, Beeze?"

He turned and looked down at her.

She knew that she flushed. "If you go to Birch's," she said determinedly, "don't go by the lower road." Irene, leaving their house, had gone down that way. . . .

Beeze laughed a little and flipped Connie's chin with his fingertip. "I saw them down there this noon when I came up here. They were in Adams' car, all cozy-cozy. I saw her go back that way when she had paid her call on us. I suppose she knows we saw her. Both times."

"Beeze . . ." Connie was not very good at interfering in other people's affairs. And she had certainly bungled this well-meant intent.

Beeze bent over to look into her face. "Are you worried about *them?*" he asked. "Upset?"

Connie should say that she was if Beeze would accept that excuse for her jitters. . . .

She couldn't do it. "No," she said. "I worry about Birch, of course, but . . ."

Beeze straightened. "I don't give a hoot about Irene, either," he declared. "But you are upset, Connie. . . ."

"I know it," she said wanly. "I know it, and I wish—" She broke off and rubbed her bare arms.

He touched her shoulder. "What, Connie?" he asked intently. "What is it you wish?"

She could only stand shaking her head, engulfed in panic, terrified again of what was going to happen, of what must happen. . . .

8

BIRCH BUELL was the middle brother of the three, and even Connie was ready to say that he might be the "nicest" of them. By this she meant—well, he had not Beeze's disarming charm, nor the drive of John, the surgeon, but he was a kind, friendly, dependable man. His brothers had those qualities, too, but Birch worked at them.

His own description was, "I don't have Beeze's nerve, nor John's brains, so I have to work at the things I do have."

In any case, he was a nice guy. And on that particular evening, a puzzled one.

For one thing, he had not yet heard of the "trouble" up the hill when he called John around eight-thirty to talk to him on a matter of business. Birch's office took care of the properties which the brothers owned singly or in common.

Connie answered the telephone, told him that John had been called to the hospital. Could she help? Well, no, not if it was business, she couldn't. How was Birch? She, in turn, was all right, and if the children were any better, no one could stand them around.

"And then," Birch told himself, "she asked me the most surprising question. At the time, I supposed she was reading some book or other. I didn't ask— I should have. But Connie asked me, out of the blue, this question. Why should she want to know about common-law wives, what they were—if there were children, what were their rights? I did manage to ask her why she was interested, and she said some woman she knew had brought up the matter.

"I answered her, not too precisely—we spoke of other things, and I hung up." She did not mention the man who had taken sick at their house, and about whom Beeze told him later.

Beeze had decided not to stop in when he left John's. He had gone instead directly to the Riddles' and had made himself useful, then eaten dinner alone. It was almost nine when he finally came to Birch's and told him about the "guy" up at the big house.

Birch was astonished. Connie had not mentioned him, Irene had not—if she knew.

"She knew," said Beeze.

"But who is the fellow? Why didn't they send him to the County Hospital? John can't take in every tramp who collapses on his property."

"The man looks like a tramp," said Beeze, "and he smelled like a tramp, but I get the idea, Birch, that he is *not* a tramp."

"Now what in hell do you mean by that?"

"I don't know. It's more a feeling—"

"Tell me again. Just what happened."

"You're sounding like a trial lawyer."

"That's all right. I am a trial lawyer. So tell me."

"Well, most of it happened, really, before I came around. You see . . ."

And Beeze told him. What had happened last night, guessing at what had happened before he got to the house. This man had got in, he said, and had frightened Connie. "I never saw anyone so terrified! The thought of him can still put her into a spin. But last night, her first thought was of the kids. . . ."

"Was she alone?"

"She was alone. Damnedest thing. John provides her with servants—she sends 'em off. Well, anyway, she managed to get the man outside—she says he wanted to use the bathroom—this was after she'd given him a drink or two. He stank of gin when I handled him."

"You . . . ? Well, go on. I'll ask questions later."

"Okay. She got him out, and he collapsed on the outside stairs that lead down to the terrace. Heart attack of some kind. John came home just about then, and was working over the guy when I showed up."

"Didn't he call the police?"

"No. He and Connie had brought the fellow inside to the couch in the playroom. When I came, I had to help put him to bed. Connie sat with him all last night. . . ."

"Still scared?"

"She was still scared at five o'clock this evening."

"Do you think he'd raped her, Beeze?"

"Oh . . ." Beeze stared at his brother. "Oh, he couldn't have!" Meaning, he could not bear the thought.

Birch shrugged. "It happens," he said. "Well—go on. What did she tell? Does she know who the man is?"

"If so, she isn't telling. He didn't have any identification. I helped undress him, and we looked. There may be a car parked somewhere, maybe down on the river road."

He told about Dr. Rinke, and Mrs. Toomey. Birch listened,

shaking his head. John, he said, should have called the police the minute he got home.

"And let the guy die of his heart attack?"

No, that would not have been like John. "But since he began to care for him, Beeze, now he cannot abandon the case."

"Does he have to go on caring for him in his home?"

"No. And I'll talk to brother John about that."

"Since he scares Connie so, I'd think John would want to get him out."

"Maybe he doesn't know that the guy scares her."

"Oh . . ."

"Even doctors, as husbands, get so they don't see what's happening to their wives."

"Your arguments for marriage overwhelm me."

Birch smiled wryly. "My arguments on that subject wouldn't overwhelm anyone. Do you have any guesses about this man?"

"Either he did more to Connie when he came into the house than she is telling—she has a nasty bruise on her forearm, and he may have put it there. This evening, when John came home, she changed into a long-sleeved dress."

"Mhmmmn. Or. . . ?"

"Or he is someone she does know. I had one wild idea. . . ."

"How wild?"

"Well—She's never mentioned a brother, but I wonder if this character might be . . . You know? Perhaps he disgraced his family, was in jail, escaped—or something like that."

Birch laughed. "That's wild, all right," he agreed.

"She's scared. You should see her."

"I'll get up there tomorrow. Meanwhile, I'll take your word for it."

"I hope, after this, she keeps her doors locked and someone in the house with her."

"Maybe she'll do what you say. But only last night, I told her the same thing."

"And she didn't listen."

"Maybe she did. Maybe she locked the doors."

"If this chap *broke* in, that's more serious, isn't it?"

Birch shook his head. "I'd say it is serious enough," he conceded.

Beeze departed without seeing Irene, though he could hear her in another part of the house. She had a radio, or TV, going softly, perhaps with the door closed.

When he left, Birch picked up the telephone. Irene came in while he was still talking. He wished she had not; he had been hoping to start his investigation of John's house guest as quietly as possible. Having Irene know about it would not be quiet at all.

But he went on and asked his friend—another attorney—a criminal lawyer—just how one would go about investigating a person.

Yes, a man. Though wouldn't the same moves apply to a woman?

Yes, he could get fingerprints—and, of course, a description—

Irene took a magazine and sat down on the couch. She had spent the past hour arranging her red hair into a series of thick loops about her face, topped with a chignon. She now felt of her masterpiece, wondering if Birch would notice it. She supposed the person he planned to investigate was herself. But what was there to investigate? Did he plan to have her shadowed, watched, trailed?

Probably.

Probably, too, he had seen her with Cliff. Today.

She had spent a large part of today arguing with the man. And Birch, somehow, had seen her. This, after her promise made only the night before, to try to do better, to try to be a proper wife.

Birch should have done more than see her with Cliff. He should have listened in on the things she had been saying to Adams.

She remembered. She'd gone down the hill with Ciff that morning, as had been arranged yesterday, but not ready, she told him at once, for the day's expedition which they had planned. No. Overnight she had had a change of heart, an onrush of good sense, an attack of conscience. . . .

"Birch put his foot down," said Cliff wryly.

"Well, he promised to."

Adams was a cool one. "What were his terms?"

"Stop seeing you, or give him a divorce."

"So what's your problem?" He'd kissed her then, without any cooperation from her.

He had protested about that, but she insisted that she did want to talk to him. She reminded him that when she first knew him—eight or ten years ago—she had decided that Birch was the best bet for the long race. She still thought he was.

Cliff had then tried to persuade her, in his own way. They sat in his car; they went for a short drive. They ate lunch at one of the restaurant-bars on the river road. And they talked. She repeatedly told him that Birch knew of their affair, that he wanted a divorce.

"Good!" he said when they reached that point again in the

circle. "It's what you want, isn't it?"

"No. It is not."

"You might have known he'd find out sooner or later, cookie."

She had no answer for that. She might have known. Cliff used various means to persuade her. And he was a persuasive man. "Give him his divorce," was the theme of what he said. "Then you and I— I'll show you what a marriage can be, cookie. It'll be your kind of marriage—not the five-room house you have now, your dishwasher and central air conditioning. Not your trip once a year to the American Bar Association meeting. . . ."

Irene had laughed at that. And Cliff thought he had won. "You know you had no business ever marrying a solid citizen, Irene," he told her. "From the start there were two strikes against that working."

Which was just what John had told Birch, and what Birch had repeated to Irene. But Cliff's saying the same thing made her mad.

She told Cliff that she would "think about it."

"When will you tell me?"

"Next time I see you."

He had let her go home then, but an hour later he called. He was leaving for the west coast, he said. He would be gone a week or more; he'd like to know how things stood between himself and Irene before—

"I can't talk over the phone."

"I could—"

"Don't come to the house! Look. I'll meet you down at the river. At the boat dock where we were this morning. Five o'clock?"

He had agreed. She had detoured past Connie's, found out

about the sick man from the gardener and Cleve and Emma, and nothing at all from Connie and Beeze—but, dear Lord, if they could patronize her now, how would they consider her should she and Birch . . . ?

"I won't ever be respectable with Cliff Adams," she told herself aloud. And she had gone straight down the hill to tell him exactly that. There was some chance she might learn to be like Connie and the Buells. She said again that she had married Birch in the first place with some such ambition in mind.

"You'll never make it," Adams assured her.

"I can try. Birch would help me.

"Oh, sure he would. Sure, he *would!*" He was going to get nasty.

"He would," Irene insisted.

"Maybe he wants a divorce on his own account."

"I don't think so. Birch is the kind to want to have things work out right. Do you know he blames himself for the mess our marriage has become?"

"Smart guy," said Cliff, stealing a look at his watch.

"He is smart," Irene agreed. "And various other things. You know? I am just beginning to realize that Birch is something rather wonderful."

Cliff yawned. "He is," he said indifferently. "That's why he's not the right man for dopes like you—and me."

Irene nodded. "That's too bad, isn't it?" she asked gloomily.

"Maybe. Now, look, Irene." He sat sideways in the car seat, facing her; he put his hand on her forearm. "You've been considering what a divorce will mean to you. You'd have to give up being Mrs. Birch Buell, and all that crap. You say you admire this Birch. Have you ever considered giving that right guy a break?"

She stared at him. Sandy hair, steady gray eyes, his freckles. The way his smile wreathed his mouth with little curved lines. All around . . .

"I'll marry you," Cliff had reminded her.

9

THE WEEK END was got through somehow. Connie met it with apprehension, but enough wariness that she did not try to force things. Saturday, Sunday—nothing really happened. Scottie, and Toomey, were isolated in the guest suite downstairs. Scottie was "coming along," though still sleeping most of the time. Gradually, she knew, he would become alert. Then he would talk, then he would tell who he was—and there was nothing Connie could think of to do to prevent this. She would have to wait him out. . . . She settled into uneasy watchfulness, coming to the point where she almost wished he would talk. Meanwhile she would try to hold on to her nerves, keep her face serene. . . .

She may have thought she was maintaining a level of calm. But she did not appear so to her husband. He noted the way her hands would clench, the way she would bite her lip and be careful in what she said. He noted the strain—it was almost desperation—within her love for the children and for himself. She would alternately cling to him and respond to him—then draw back and hold herself aloof, her face white with strain.

She acted like a child with a guilty secret. But that was never Connie! Something had happened. . . .

He blamed the stranger who had come to their home. What had the man done to his girl? He, too, saw the bruise on her arm. "I played too rough with Grey," she answered his question. But John did not believe her. He considered questioning her further, and more sharply, more specifically—but the panic in her eyes, the hurt . . . Perhaps he could find other ways.

Meanwhile, he was most concerned for her.

As he drove into the city early on Monday morning, he thought about it all.

The telephone beside his bed had rung promptly at six forty-five as, lying there, half awake in the shadows of early morning, he had expected it to do.

"It is now six forty-five," said Miss Danford. She herself would still be at home. John listened, tightening his senses to comprehend, to remember.

The bedroom was in half-darkness, though the sun was up and, out of doors, a bird was singing. The night before, Connie had drawn the draperies, for privacy, and against the early dawn.

"At eight oclock," Miss Danford's voice told the doctor, "you are at University for a lobectomy. At eleven-thirty you are at Mercy for a conference, and you have a mitral stenosis there at one. At four you are at your office. At eight-thirty you have a meeting of the Medical Society. That is all."

"Will you be home for dinner?" Connie asked drowsily as he put down the phone.

"I hope to be, but I'll have to go out again about eight."

While he showered and shaved, he thought about Connie's nervousness. During the week end she would not leave the house, not even to go to church, nor to attend a small party on Sunday afternoon.

He dressed and went downstairs for his car; he drove it against the morning sunlight, his eyes shielded behind dark glasses. He reached the lot, locked the car, and walked, fast, toward the hospital door—a tall man, his head carried well on his straight shoulders.

Connie had tried to conceal her state of nerves, making a noticeable effort to be the woman she had become as John's wife, loving, responsive, thoughtful in all the little things. . . .

He signed the register. John Grey Buell, M.D. And—

"Excuse me, Dr. Buell," said the receptionist. "Your patient's wife and son would like to talk to you."

He preferred not to start a surgical day in that way, but he turned at once to meet the woman in her late fifties, and her broad-shouldered son, about thirty, who were standing against the wall. These people had their own worries.

The woman put her hand out toward the doctor. "We wanted to wish you luck," she said, trying to smile. But the fear in her face left no room for it.

"Oh, look," Dr. Buell said warmly, "you mustn't worry. We are going to take good care of him."

"I know you are," said the son.

"Think of this," said John. "I am not worried, so there's no point in you two . . ." He smiled at the little woman in her dark blue dress.

"God bless you, Doctor," she said, still trying to smile.

Dr. Buell nodded and went down the hall. He had spoken the truth. Still a "young surgeon," John Buell, ten years ago, had lost the tension which had used to grip him before an operation, the anticipation, the thinking about everything that could go wrong. After opening chests some four thousand times, he no longer tightened up over a single "job," nor played it over and over. Now he had his procedures and his team so perfectly systematized that each move was almost reflex. He refined his technique all the time, refined and refined it, but worry? No. That was gone—along with some of the excitement and the exhilaration, of course.

But he remembered the tension, and had recognized just that in Connie the last couple of days. Being a gay companion for the children, welcoming the brothers when they dropped in, and the friends too who had come, even playing croquet with them and John, she would have minutes when she would stand with a smile frozen on her lips—and she would rub the goose bumps which had appeared on her slender, sun-browned arms. *Why?*

He pushed the elevator button marked O.R. and felt the surge of the rising cage. Toomey was on the case at home. What had Connie to shiver about?

He strode down the hall into the doctors' locker room.

"Full roster of great surgeons, I see," he said cordially to the men in the room.

"Good morning, Doctor," said George Bennet.

John glanced at him and slipped out of his jacket. "Hi, Benny," he answered

Some of the half-dozen men were undressing in front of their lockers, some, already in the shapeless washed-green two-piece suits and caps, were sitting about, their masks dangling. There was talk, some joking. John hung his coat on a hanger and took off his tie. . .

Last evening Connie would not walk with him down to the river, though it was a trip they often made, and enjoyed, together. "I don't think we should leave the children," she had said, which was a feeble excuse, unless she was more afraid of the sick man than would seem sensibly possible.

Stripped to his shorts and socks, John put his watch and wallet on the bench so he would not forget them. The trouble was, Connie was not being sensible. He got into his own "pajamas" and put on the gauze cap, smoothing it down over his short brown hair.

"Very pretty, Doctor," said one of the surgeons, passing him, and John frowned a little. "Oh, thanks, Akins!" he said then, recovering. "Thanks a lot!" The sick stranger in his home had him acting oddly, too.

He took a mask, shook it out, and tied the bottom strings around his neck. He put on his half-glasses and slid his feet into the open-backed white leather operating shoes.

"Well," he said, slamming his locker door and picking up his valuables, "you other famous surgeons can sit around in here and talk about girls and taxes. I have work to do."

Benny followed him out into the hall in time for them both to wait for a stretcher to be brought out of the elevator.

"Is that our man?" John asked, his voice low.

"No. You'll remember him when you see the X-rays."

"I used to remember them all," John said. He went over to the desk, put his wallet and watch into a Manila envelope, sealed it, and handed it back to the nurse, who tore off the identifying tag and gave it to him with a smile. He pushed the slip of paper up under his cap.

"I used to remember all the patients," he began again to Dr. Bennet. "Their faces, the way they handled their fears, how they earned their living for what sized families. I knew about their anxieties and their hopes. . . ."

"And you found you couldn't carry such a load, day after day," said Benny, "as you got busier."

"I remember one man who had never spent a night away from his wife . . ." mused John. "His son had talked him into coming to the hospital. And I lost him. I remember standing at the end of the hall, afterwards, just looking down at a tree."

"It's better this way," said his assistant.

Better for the surgeon, he meant. Just to hear what he had to know, and not let the patients talk to him very much, tell him about themselves.

John was not sure it was better. Easier on him, perhaps.

"John," said Bennet, "here are the pictures."

John walked into the operating room, said "Hello" to the anesthetist, to the scrub nurse, and to the floating nurse; he followed Benny over to where the X-rays were clipped in the lighted panels of the side wall. He saw the shadow, almost the size of an orange, in the upper lobe of the left lung, half hidden by the heart shadow. "Oh, yes," he said. "I remember the man."

Yesterday, Connie had kept the family, and the visitors, up in the living room, on the deck there, or at the far end of the lower terrace, away from the sickroom, though in that big house, they would not have disturbed their patient. John was puzzled!

About that patient at home—able to talk a little now, but seemingly disinclined—and about the patient who, within minutes, would be brought into this operating room. He had been scared, as all men were scared who began to spit blood, whose wife had noticed his loss of breath, his failing appetite, whose wife had nagged him into seeing the doctor.

John had tried to reassure this man. "It's as much as my reputation is worth not to take care of you," he had said, or something like it. He was accustomed to reassuring these frightened, big men who had always been healthy, able to work. . . . The patient had to believe in his doctor, or he would quit when the doctor needed his help.

John had talked to this patient, had questioned him and assured him that what ailed him could be fixed. He had then met the wife and reassured her, joking with her a little.

But he and Dr. Bennet had known immediately that they had cancer on their hands. "I heard the wheeze the minute I put the stethoscope near the lesion," John had said. That squeaky-door sound, the symptoms, the history . . . "I remember him," he said now to Benny.

He walked over to the tape rack, tore off a four-inch strip of half-inch tape, fastened it to his forehead, then he ran it across the bridge of his glasses, and down to his nose to hold the glasses firmly in place. He walked out into the hall.

The patient lay on his bed there, with the sheet tucked primly under his chin. "Good morning," the doctor said to him. "Were you waiting for someone?"

The man managed a faint smile. "You," he said, his voice croaking.

John lifted the left wrist, not to count the pulse—though he could hit it without a watch, and not miss by more than five beats—but to check on the regularity and the strength of that pulse.

Yesterday he had taken the pulse of the man he had at home, and he had tried to read the stranger's face and eyes. That man had been watching him, too, and he had not spoken. If he had, he probably would not have said to John Buell what this pre-op now said. "I want you to know that I trust you, Doctor," he said.

John laid the wrist back on the bed, drew the sheet up. "That's why I studied medicine," he said, "to have chaps like you trust me."

He spoke the truth. That was why he had studied medicine, and worked the long hours, the long years, to become a successful, which meant skilled, surgeon. He smiled down at the man. "They'll stick you with a needle any minute now," he said "and the next you'll know will be when you are back in your room, complaining because the nurse isn't pretty enough."

He picked up the large Manila envelope from the foot of the bed, and went over to a window where he could read the reports. He checked hemoglobin and urinalysis, the liver test and the electrocardiogram. All organs were functioning normally. When he turned away from the window, the bed was being pushed into o.r. He gave the envelope to the nurse at the door.

The man at home . . . John did not allow himself the luxury of liking or disliking a patient. But that fellow—he had only Connie's reaction to the man on which to base his growing animosity. The fellow could talk now, and he had not been very responsive, but otherwise his relationship to the doctor had been passive. John had done what he wanted to do for him; the patient had had no choice. . . .

Still . .

He went in to scrub, peeled the adhesive tape from his nose, lifted his mask, and fastened the tape on it. He knotted the two strings of the mask, tying them above his cap. Then, with only his eyes showing, he stepped to the deep square sink next to Dr. Bennet, who lifted his eyes briefly to his face. John nodded. He reached for the brush, found the foot pedal with his toe, squirted antiseptic soap on his hands and, under the bright cone of jetting water, he began to scrub rhythmically, following the pattern, first the hands, then the forearms—five minutes. He no longer had to look at the clock, or count. He had been doing this four or five, sometimes ten, times a week for too many years. So long that the scrubbing and the rubber gloves had made his hands soft; John hated to shake hands with other men.

Last night—*scrub, scrub*—he had made love to Connie. In a way that was not usual with his tender, loving girl, she had, at first, been reluctant, and then she had clung to him with a fierceness, an intensified show of the desperate, anxious love which he had detected earlier in her affection for the children.

"Hey, hey!" he had protested. "Take it easy, sweetheart. Leave some for tomorrow."

Her eyes had fairly blazed at him. "What if there is no tomorrow?" she had demanded. "What *if?*"

Frowning, John now finished with his hands, his arms, first one, then the other; with them dripping, he pushed the o.r. door open with his right shoulder, and holding his hands upward, the palms toward himself, he went over to the table which held the sterile gowns and the folded towels. He picked up a square of green linen and dried his hands and arms, still thinking about Connie—and the situation at home. How was he going to handle it?

The scrub nurse came over and shook out a gown; he slipped into it, and the floating nurse tied it in back. He took another towel, slit the package of powder, dusted his hands, and thrust them into the gloves. He could remember the first time he had ever put on rubber gloves before surgery. The nurse had had to help him. That hitch would not bother him now, but then his confusion had been agonizing.

Should he move the man at home out of the house? Should he be patient with Connie, wait and see if she would not come around, relax, and tell him of her own accord just what had happened to terrify her so?

He turned to look at the patient, now on the table, under the lights. The upper half of his body was uncovered, pale, thin. The man was under the anesthesia, the intratracheal tube was down his windpipe, and the anesthetist was taping it to his left cheek. John watched her.

"How are we doing, Mollie Bee?" he asked her.

"Fine, Doctor. We're just fine."

John said "Good morning" to the intern.

"Good morning, Dr. Buell," the young doctor answered. In five more years, the intern would be saying "Good morning, *sir*." John could wait for that honor, though the years did not bother him much. Not half as much as . . .

Could he afford to wait to see what would happen at home? Because, what *would* happen?

He stood there, tall, priestlike, his gloved hands folded in front of him, and watched the intern and Dr. Bennet turn the patient on his right side with his right arm, the intravenous tube rising from it, out along the arm board. The left arm was folded up out of the way. The right leg was bent at the knee —for stability—and the left extended straight. A pillow was put under the head, and one between the legs. Then Benny and the intern anchored the body, pulling wide strips of adhesive tight across the hips, crossing them, then fastening them to the table. The intern began to soap the patient's chest, and John walked over to take another look at the X-rays. One thing was certain; he was going to make the guy at home talk to him, and Connie, too. He needed the man's name; he needed to stop being concerned for his wife.

But— For now he would consider only the wall of this room and the shadow on that X-ray plate; it lay in the lung field, next to the heart.

He walked back to the table. "Don't scrub our patient clear away," he told the industrious intern. "I don't know where I'd find another on such short notice."

"No, sir," said the intern, looking at him, the swab held in midair.

"Very good," said the doctor in charge. "I think you can paint him now."

If the intern knew what he should know, he would paint the correct field, dipping into the pan of disinfectant, swabbing the back and the chest pink-orange with Merthiolate.

"That will do it," John said by way of commendation. The table, he determined, was at the proper height for him not to end the day with a pain across his shoulders. The scrub nurse stepped up and swung the instrument tray into position. He held out his left hand, and she pressed a scalpel into it. He turned it in his hand, and with the back of it he scratched the skin, marking it, under the left breast, bringing it up in a big C, shifting the knife to his right hand, and finishing behind the shoulder blade. Then he made two small marks, intersecting his scratch, about twelve inches apart.

"When we put him back together," he told the intern, "that will show us where the edges should go."

"Yes, sir," said the intern, looking a bit doubtful.

"I don't want the privilege of living my life over," John thought, "and being an intern again. This kid, before we drape the body, can see only the ugly aging of it. While, at my stage of the game, I find it beautiful, everything orderly, clean and functional." He made a frame of towels around the scratch, then, over the whole body, he and Dr. Bennet and the intern spread the green thoracotomy sheet, with its white-trimmed opening precisely in place.

"The intern won't see any beauty here," thought the surgeon, "because to him, under the sheet, still lies a man, and pain. But Benny and I know what we are doing here, and what can be done."

He and "Benny" clamped the sheet so that one end of it extended up above the man's head and the anesthetist seated on her stool. " 'By, Mollie," the surgeon said, waiting for her to lift her eyes. He nodded. "See you later."

She nodded. "I'll be here."

"You'd better be," John chuckled.

"Is everybody set?" he asked his team.

"Right, John," said Dr. Bennet.

"Yes, sir, " said the intern.

The scrub nurse echoed him.

"What time is it?"

"Eight twenty-six, Doctor," said the float.

"Okay. Then let's go." He reached his right hand across. "Knife," he said.

The handle of the scalpel pressed upon his palm, and his hand closed upon it. With the sure and easy precision of four thousand operations done before this one, his knife point followed the scratch which he had made earlier. The pink-painted skin rolled back, revealing the yellow fat layer and the tough white tissue that lay over the muscles.

"The bigger the incision," he said to his tight-faced intern, "the bigger the fee we doctors can charge. Did you know that?"

"No, sir," said the young man.

"I have to loosen up this boy," thought the surgeon. "Him, and Mollie, and the scrub nurse, or they'll be exhausted by the time I need them for the big job."

"You realize what a help it is for the patient to have kept

himself thin," he said aloud. Across the table, Benny was beginning to clamp the stockinet into place along the edge of the wound. John held out his hand, and the nurse gave him his own stockinet, which molded to the wound better than the old linen skin towels.

"Where did you go to med school?" he asked the intern.

"Rush Medical, sir."

"Then you have watched Dr. Norton do this job?"

"Yes, sir."

"I've seen men standing in the hall there, hoping for a chance to watch him do a lobe. *Ah-ha!* There's a bleeder. Sneaky thing thought it could hide." He sponged and saw that all the small, spurting vessels had been clamped.

There would be a hundred or more bleeders. Going in was really only a matter of cutting, tying off, cutting—skin, tissue, and muscle. Then the ribs, and the chest. He held the clamp; Benny tied the knot. Then Benny did the same for him.

He stopped the intern who was cutting a thread. "You hold those scissors like a woman," he told the young doctor. "Here! Watch me." He extended his hand, and the scrub nurse gave him a pair of scissors. He held them for the intern to see, with the thumb and ring finger in the eyes, the middle finger to the side, and the index finger down the length of them like a pointer. "Stronger that way," said the surgeon. "You can cut anything. Knife!"

Starting at the triangle where the back and shoulder muscles joined, he cut through the white, tough tissue, turned his left hand palm up, and slid his fingers into the opening. Spreading them, he cut the first muscles forehanded, watching them snap back, then he did the second set backhanded. With each cut, sure of what he was doing, he went through to the rib covering, the periosteum. A young doctor had to learn not to scratch, but to cut. John had had to learn. This intern would need to.

So long as he scratched, the operation was running the doctor. A man had to learn to go down in, and lick it, be the master.

"Do you go to the horse races, Doctor?" John asked the intern.

"Well, sometimes, sir. I enjoy them."

"Mhmmmn. Well, what we are doing here is something like horse racing. You need two speeds. You start out flashy, quick. Out the gate, running well, always the same; it gets to be automatic. That's the way with a chest opening. We just go into it, one, two, three. Then," said the surgeon, sponging, "when we get inside, we settle down to the steady job. We round the curve, we come into the stretch, and we call up our reserve power for the burst. D'you see?"

"Yes, sir. I think so."

The metal retractors were going in now to enlarge the chest opening. The scrub nurse was wringing saline solution out of the wet pack, then handing it to Benny, who placed the wet gauze over and around the wound to protect it from the metal retractors. John placed the next one and Benny hooked the curved end of the first retractor over the hot pack, around and under the shoulder blade. He placed and handed the second retractor to the intern. He and Benny pulled, and the wound began to widen.

"Oh, come on, fellows," John cried. "Lift that thing— You two need some physical conditioning, that's for sure."

He reached up under the shoulder blade and found the muscle attached to the second rib; moving his fingers down over the ribs, he counted them. ". . . three, four, five . . ."

He took the retractor from his assistant, and Dr. Bennet reached in and counted. "Right!" he said to Dr. Buell.

"How're we doing, Mollie?" John asked the anesthetist.

"All right, Doctor. Pulse eighty-six, pressure one fifteen over eighty-five."

"Knife," said the surgeon.

He cut through the tough, adhering periosteum and dropped the scalpel into the towel. Danford handed him the elevator, and he used it to scrape the periosteum out of his way. "Good girl," he murmured.

"I've had practice, Doctor," said his scrub nurse primly.

"That always helps." Practice was what let John push the periosteum over and under the rib with just two moves; the gray white arch of the rib cage enlarged, cleanly, almost bloodlessly.

"Beautiful," breathed Dr. Bennet. "You must have practiced, too."

"Just lucky, I guess," said the surgeon. "Could I please have the rib cutter?"

The rib cutter was double action, and he severed the rib at one side, and then the other. The scrub nurse took it and wrapped it in a sterile towel. "Sponge count?" asked John, meeting her eyes.

"Correct, sir."

"Good." He lifted his voice. "Wake up, Mollie," he called. "Do a little work. Will you please breathe for our man here while I cut the pleura?"

"I'm awake, Doctor," called the doctor behind the sheet. She would turn on the automatic respirator.

With his scissors, John reached in and severed the inner periosteum, and then the elastic lining of the chest cavity, destroying the chest vacuum. But Mollie had kept the lung from collapsing; he could hear the click and hiss of the respirator. She would be watching her dials and feeling the pressure in her anesthetic bag.

"Rib spreader."

It felt loose; he turned it over and tightened the wing nut. His eyes questioned Miss Danford.

"Isn't it all right?" she asked.

"Now it is, yes." He placed the spreader between the fourth and sixth ribs, and set it. Benny gave the handle four turns, and the opening began to enlarge.

"Good," said John. Again with his scissors he split the muscle between the fourth and what was left of the fifth rib. Now the ribs should not break. He liked to do as little damage to the patient as possible.

"Crank him," he said then, and Bennet turned the handle until the area opened, exposing the lung, pink and purple and black, enclosed within the steel frame of the spreader. The marbleized lung rose and fell, controlled by Mollie behind the sheet.

"What time is it?" asked the surgeon.

"Eight forty-seven, Doctor."

Sometimes he could open in twelve minutes—with a skinny patient and everyone on the team loose and relaxed.

"Drop the pressure a little, Mollie," he said. "I want enough collapse to see what's wrong with this gentleman."

"Yes, Doctor."

This, *this minute*, was it! He reached in. Everyone in the room was watching. Even Mollie, still feeling her pressure bag, half stood to peer over the sheet. What had up to then been only symptoms and a shadow on an X-ray film, now lay under the doctor's right hand.

He felt the lung, normal and pliable, and then, right at the edge of it, the beginning of a hardness, a spreading patch. Slowly he followed it to the root, which was hard, then down to the heart, and there was the leatherlike hardness on the pericardium itself. His hand went down to the spleen and to the left lobe of the liver. They were normal.

"I can take it now," he thought, "the whole lung, the lymph nodes, and that hard part of the pericardium, denude the adjacent structure—and my man could die right here on the table or in the next few days. *Or* I could close up, send him back to his wife and son with the only hope lying in the new chemicals, in cobalt or radium. . . . The choice lies right here."

The only sound in the room was the *tick, hiss, tick, hiss* of the respirator. John turned the lung to expose the waxy, yellow-gray growth. He looked up at Bennet. "This patient," he said aloud, "had suspected for six months that he had cancer of the lung. He tried to forget it. Now . . ." He stepped aside to let Bennet explore.

"He's not sixty," John thought. "If we take the lung, his heart will stand it. The right lung is in good shape, and does most of the work anyway. If we get away with this, he won't be a wheelchair cripple."

"Well?" he said aloud to his assistant. "Can he stand a pneumonectomy?"

"I'd say yes," said Dr. Bennet.

At these times, John always thought of himself as the patient. If this were his body . . . If he were almost sixty . . . Grey would be in college, Corey sweet with her first love, and Connie . . . "I'd not want them to close me up," he decided now.

He nodded to Benny. "I'd say yes, too."

If a surgeon did only nice, clean cases he would not only

forget how to do the tough ones, but he would lose his nerve as well. It was only from the hard ones that a surgeon learned; it was from them he earned a reward. The key to this job . . .

"If we can get a clean artery," he said aloud, "we can get this out."

The strategy would be to tie off the pulmonary artery, not telling the anesthetist. If there was no distress or deterioration, he would know that the patient could live with only one lung. If there was trouble, well, he'd have to close up. He worked with concentration. Vagus nerve, largyngeal nerves held out of the way, pulmonary artery isolated. "I think we'll get it," he told Bennet.

Forceps, and heavy silk ties, using a right angle—the first knot didn't hold. The third one did, and he asked for the pulse.

Inside another man's chest, a stranger's chest, a surgeon took over that man's pulse, the rhythm of it—and he noticed any single small break in that rhythm.

"Pulse one hundred, pressure one twenty over eighty."

"Good." Now he could get back to work. For five minutes he prepared the veins for separation and heard nothing from Mollie.

"How're you doing?" he asked finally.

"Pulse ninety-six, pressure one ten over eighty."

He knew he could do it. The patient was holding his own. Having done this job so often, the surgeon knew that he could do this one, and the patient would live. He thought about the first surgeon who ever had dared to remove a cancerous lung. John had studied and worked under a man who had been resident for that doctor. A brave man, a benefactor of first quality. What had it taken in courage, imagination, and dedication to do that first operation?

He went to work, separating the veins, tying them. He asked for light. The scrub nurse offered to notify pathology.

"Tell 'em it will be fifteen minutes," John said. If this thing were not so obvious, he would have waited on pathology. "I'll want them to take a good look at the lymph nodes."

He asked for a bronchial clamp, and for the lung to be collapsed a little. Dr. Bennet held the lung with three forceps. John clamped the bronchus, cutting through the hard whiteness between the two clamps. He took the three lung forceps from Benny and handed them to the intern.

"Hold these in both hands, Doctor," he said. "Firmly. Now lift!"

The lung came out, the intern holding it. He looked at the surgeon, eyes wide and round—startled.

John's eyes crinkled at the corners. "You came in here to do surgery, Doctor," he said. "You have just removed a lung."

The intern nodded. "Me and Dr. Norton," he said. Then, more softly, "Me and Dr. Buell." He looked up. "Thank you, Doctor," he said faintly. He dropped the lung into the pan which the scrub nurse held.

John glanced at the clock. It was ten twenty-nine.

He waited while Bennet drained the area of blood, then he began to remove the chain of lymph nodes. He was pleased to note, and point out, that these were a normal black.

"Do you want them to go to pathology, Doctor?" asked the scrub nurse.

"Sure. Let them be as pleased as I am. Mark this sub-aortic and put it in a separate pan. And will somebody call my office and say I won't make that conference but will do the heart on time."

He asked for a knife, fine sutures, and long forceps. "This will be a bad bronchus to close," he murmured, as if telling himself. "Cartilage of the wall is as hard as bone. Mollie?"

"Yes, sir."

"Take ten breaths, then stop."

Following this procedure, ten breaths, stop, suture, tie—ten breaths—he closed the bronchus, the sutures squeaking against his rubber gloves. He asked for a saline wash, tipped the liquid into the chest, covering the stub. "Press hard on your bag, Mollie," he directed. "Are you pushing hard?"

"Yes, sir."

There were no bubbles rising to the surface of the saline.

"I'm still pushing, Dr. Buell."

"You've done fine. Now you can stop." No contaminated air would get into the chest.

Next he must work on that patch which had reached the heart. Benny and the intern were using the tonsil suckers to clear the saline from the area. When they had finished, John took the scissors and worked right against the heart, giving himself about an inch of safety. He cut the cancerous rectangle away. The heart lay bare and he must patch the pericardium. The pleura was smoother and more fragile than the heart's natural covering; he cut a patch of this material to match the size of the hole he had made. It looked much like the stuff of the gloves he wore. He spread it on a towel.

"Wipe for Dr. Buell," said Benny.

John waited, not having realized that he was sweating. The float swabbed at his forehead with the gauze. "How're we doing, Mollie?" he asked.

"Pressure holding—one ten over eighty."

That was very good. "I'll need a half hour to close."

"Yes, sir."

He put thread through each corner of his patch, held it up by one corner, the other strings dangling. He laid it on the hole, against the heart. "Give me a little tension," he told Benny. The assistant grasped two of the threads. John sewed each corner in place, then stitched around the whole edge. "I wouldn't let my wife do this kind of job on the seat of my Sunday pants," he said, and the float giggled.

But his patch would hold, and keep the heart from popping out into the chest. In ten days the patch would have healed into a part of the heart tissue.

The pathologist at the door announced to him that he had a carcinoma of the lung. "Thank you," said Dr. Buell politely.

"A couple of those nodes merit microscopic examination."

"I got them all, good and bad," John told him. "There's a bleeder, Benny." He held the clamp.

While Benny worked, John asked the intern if he was familiar with the symptoms of this case. "Did you know—do you know that other diseases can cause similar symptoms?"

"Yes, sir. TB, pneumonia . . ."

"And arthritis, bursitis, gall bladder disease. However, this man wasn't fooled about what he had. Though he still delayed six months."

"Yes, sir."

John again filled the cavity with saline, and there were no bubbles. He waited for the fluid to be sucked out, and shook in the antibiotic powder. He put the drainage tube between the second and third rib.

"Crank him down," he said.

Dr. Bennet turned the handle of the rib spreader and took it out. The ribs were pulled back into place, the muscles restored to their natural state, and the fascia stitched.

"This was cancer," Dr. Buell instructed the intern. "We

took care of it. We can't, always. Do you know much about cancer, Doctor?"

"I—well, I have seen and helped with surgery for various kinds."

"Yes. We are learning to handle the thing, and are handling it. All except cancer of the lung, Doctor. Excessive smoking, bad air—we doctors are not keeping up with the incidence."

He broke off to ask, "How are we doing, Mollie?"

"All right, Doctor. Pulse eighty-two, pressure one twenty over eighty."

Benny was taking off the skin snaps and removing the stockinet on his side. John did the other. Then, with a straight needle, careful to match the cross marks which he had made earlier, he took the first stitch. Benny matched the other marks and began at that end. Both men worked, sewing, tying, closing the wound.

Finished, the intern cut the threads. A doubled strip of gauze was held in place with four-inch straps.

"Thank you, Dr. Bennet," said John politely. "You have made me look good this morning."

"My pleasure, Doctor."

"As a reward, I'll let you finish up here." He glanced at the clock. Eleven-forty. "I understand I'm needed over at Mercy."

"Sure, Doctor."

"Thank you, everybody."

"Yes, sir."

The float untied his gown, and he slipped out of it. He tossed his rubber gloves to her, and he stepped out into the hall, pushing his mask down, taking the adhesive from his forehead and glasses. He reclaimed his envelope of valuables and went to the empty locker room. He put his pajamas and mask and cap into the hamper. As he dressed, he felt a little tired. Not however the tiredness in every bone of his body which failure would have brought. . . .

His report made, he went downstairs and signed out, flipping the light switch beside his name. Still seated in the waiting room, he saw the patient's wife and son. He went over to them and told them that "our man" was in good shape. "He'll go to Recovery for a time, and you'll be able to see him tonight."

"God bless you, Doctor," said the wife faintly.

John's hand pressed her shoulder, and he walked away. That was what doctoring, surgery, was about, he supposed.

He crossed the hall to the phone booth and called Connie. "Is everything all right?" he asked.

Finished, he then called Mercy Hospital. "Sister," he said, "will you tell Surgery to count on my being fifteen minutes late? My wife says I must eat some lunch."

"Take care of her, Dr. Buell," said the nun. "She seems to be taking care of you."

"You're right, Sister. You're right!"

He walked fast to where he had left his car. He realized that he was hungry, having eaten nothing except the coffee and juice which Connie had brought to him that morning while he dressed. The heart before him, and office hours— Yes, he had better stop for a sandwich.

Connie was glad that John had called; she told him that things were "all right" at his home. They were, really. Mrs. Toomey was a master sergeant, and in full control. Connie stayed close to the sickroom, wanting to know what Scottie was doing or possibly saying. She could not stop his saying whatever he wanted to say, but she wanted to know. So she watched and listened.

There were diversions which interfered with this. Connie must give some attention to her home and to the children. She had made an appointment and accepted an invitation to a tea for that afternoon. These obligations could be changed, and were. Scottie was awake now, and talking some.

Midafternoon, Irene came to the house and Connie kept her up in the living room, twice excusing herself to "check on" the sitter who substituted for Madie on this, her day off. She listened to Irene talk, not really hearing her, but thinking about what Irene would and could do with the information which Scottie could give her. Of course, she herself was going to have to do something. But *Irene* . . .

Connie would have got along with Birch's wife, had she been given a chance. But Irene had been furious that John's marriage had put her and Birch out of the big house, and ever since she had held a grudge against Connie and John. She had tried to get Birch to share in her rancor, but he would have no part in it. This made her disgruntled with her husband.

Connie didn't know what Irene had wanted when she came up the hill; she didn't say, though she stayed for an hour and asked questions about the sick man.

"What made you keep him here?" she asked. "Do you know who he is?"

"Doesn't he talk?"

"Is he a neighborhood character? I mean, have you ever seen him before?"

Connie was glad to get rid of her visitor, finally, and before John came home. He had had a full day and would be tired. She hoped that she could persuade him not to attend the meeting that evening. She hoped his office would not be full. . . . She carefully planned a dinner for a warm evening and a tired man. He would want to see the children—and have a shower.

Connie smoothed the way for those things, conspiring with the sitter—an older woman whom she knew well—not to let the children be too boisterous. "Dr. Buell has done so *much* today. Whether he knows it or not, he will be tired."

John knew that he was tired, but the sight of Connie in a thin dress of pale green, the fresh clothes laid out for him, the warm shower, all served to revive him.

"Did things go well?" Connie asked him.

"Fine. Danford gave me a loose wing nut on a spreader."

"Oh, no!"

"It didn't make any difference. That job went very well. Had a new intern, but Benny is really something. I want you to help me figure out a way to get that guy to work on his own."

He showered, put on the fresh clothes, and went in to say good night to the kids. Connie allowed them fifteen minutes.

"Can we eat dinner outside?" he asked. "And do I get a drink?"

"Of course."

"I'll go down and talk to Toomey."

"Before you eat, John?" Her forehead puckered.

"Before I eat."

She followed him; she had to. But when John went into Scottie's room, he closed the bedroom door against her and Toomey. He would sit beside the bed. . . . And what would Scottie say?

Connie went along the terrace to tell Cleve to serve dinner out there. The late rays of the sun might give John . . .

"Yes, ma'am," said Cleve. "Mr. Beeze phoned and said he would like to join you, if there was dinner enough. . . ."

Connie stifled a sigh. "Did you tell him . . . ?"

"I said there would be enough dinner. I hope that was all right, ma'am?"

"Of course, Cleve. Except that Dr. Buell is tired and must go out again."

"His brother won't tire him further."

But when Connie had mixed the drinks and came down the outside stairs, Beeze was himself upset. His angry voice came loudly from the sickroom. The tray in Connie's hands began to tremble.

"Look here," Beeze was shouting. "You broke in here the other night, entered this house . . ."

Scottie was answering with surprising strength. "Wait up there, buddy!" he said. His voice had become quite husky with the years. "Wait up! I entered, but there was no *breaking* needed. That door was unlocked; I walked in."

"Why?" asked Beeze truculently.

Connie waited, feeling sick. What would Scottie say?

". . . sick," he said. "I knew this was Dr. Buell's house. I thought he would help me."

"And he will help you," said John's voice. "Mrs. Toomey!"

Connie took her tray down to the table. There had been a hardness in John's voice—but he still was being angry only because Scottie had frightened her.

The men came out, and John urged Beeze to take off his coat. "That's why I enjoy eating outside. I'd take off my shirt, but Connie would never stand for that."

Smiling, she handed him his glass.

"That's certainly a character in there," Beeze told her.

"He's better. . . ."

"Sure he is. And knows a good thing when he sees it."

"You said you had something to tell us," John reminded his brother. He reached for Connie's hand, and she sat down in the chair next to him, with her own glass of fruit juice. She had never learned to drink, which was, often, a mild joke in the family, though she thought John approved.

Beeze said that he had called at the Riddle home that afternoon.

"When do you work?" John asked him.

"Her—their grandmother was buried this morning."

"One of my bigger mistakes," John agreed.

"I've been seeing those girls, you know."

"And you wanted to know how they came out in the will."

"Oh, John!" Connie protested, and John's eyes crinkled at her.

Beeze laughed. "I didn't, but I found out," he said.

"Dinner is served, madame," said Cleve discreetly at Connie's shoulder.

They moved to the glass-topped table. There was a centerpiece of pale green grapes heaped in a silver bowl; pink rosebuds were tucked here and there among the frosty clusters. The dishes were sprigged with pink flowers; the silver shone softly. John declared he was starved, and where had Connie found the salmon?

"She's a good wife," Beeze told his brother solemnly.

"As if I didn't know. . . ."

Connie should have been pleased. A week ago their praise would have put her into a rosy glow. Tonight— She was seated where she could see the fan of light which came from the guest suite where Scottie . . .

". . . wads of money," Beeze was saying. "Everyone was expecting her to leave most of it to the twins. The grandfather's will had fixed things up for their father."

"Didn't she leave it that way?" asked John, enjoying his

dinner—the salmon steaks, the tiny new potatoes—the salad—

"Well, yes and no," said Beeze.

"Now what does that mean?"

"The damnedest thing! She left it—all but ten thousand of it—to Carrie Lee. Not to Sophia, and in the will she said that was because Sophia's mouth turned down."

"Wha-at?" asked Connie.

"You're not serious," John said, smiling.

"I am serious," Beeze insisted. "And Grandma was, too. Which means trouble for me, because now I can't marry Sophia."

"Were you planning to?" asked John.

"Sure I was."

"That's why her mouth turns down," John concluded, taking another roll. They were small, and as light as feathers.

Beeze laughed. "I had never noticed, myself, that it did turn down."

"It doesn't," said John. "Except when she is with her sister."

Beeze started to comment, then he sat thoughtful. "Hmmmm," he said.

"With only ten thousand, Grandma figured she'd step out on her own," John suggested. "Marry a poor man—an architect, maybe—raise a family—"

"You're in something of a hurry, aren't you, brother dear?" asked Beeze.

John shrugged and glanced at his watch.

Connie looked around for Cleve, and signaled for dessert to be brought with the coffee.

"Why does it turn down when she's with Carrie Lee?" she asked. "Sophia's mouth."

"There's always a dominant twin," said John. "Grandma is

going to keep it that way, and give Sophia a chance."

"I believe that is pretty complicated thinking, Doctor," his brother told him.

"You work at it."

John went to his meeting; he was to present a case, he told Connie. Beeze said he would leave, too, if Connie was not afraid?

"Why should I be?"

"Well—"

"Mrs. Toomey is here," she pointed out. "Cleve and Emma. I've a sitter with the children."

"All right then. Thank you for dinner, sweetheart. It was delish! Macaroons and lime sherbet. Who but you . . . ?"

She gave him an affectionate push. "Save your flattery for the twins, Beeze," she told him.

For a half hour she read, then she went downstairs again and asked Mrs. Toomey if she might not want to get away for an hour or two. "I'll sit with the patient."

Toomey hesitated. She had promised Dr. Buell. . . . "He's sleepin'," she said.

"Yes. I'll just sit here and read."

"I won't be gone but an hour. I would like to get my other shoes."

"Of course. And you've been so closely confined."

The nurse left in her tiny blue car, seeming to fill every cranny of it with her sturdy person.

Connie selected a chair from which she could see Scottie's head on the pillow; the night light was dim. She had not gone into his room. Determined not to let him upset her, nor even to look at him or think about him, she opened her book. If he moved, she would know it. She made her eyes follow the lines of print on the page.

That this—this *person*—could come into John Buell's home and threaten everything he cherished . . . John was a great man, a great surgeon. Today he had saved two lives with his skill, his strength, his—goodness! No, it didn't bear thinking about. She would read her story.

"Connie?"

The book slipped from her hands, and she bent over to pick it up. Scottie was looking at her. She did not rise at once.

"What do you want?" she called.

"Come in here."

"What do you want?" she asked again.

"Just to talk."

"You shouldn't talk. You've had a sedative, and—" But she got to her feet and walked into the bedroom. Scottie was probably too weak to do anything physically. And if he tried, she would run, screaming.

"I could hear you folks talking outside. The old bag said you were eating dinner."

"We were."

"What were you talking about?"

"You said you could hear."

"Not what you *said*."

"Oh, we didn't say much. We talked about some friend of Dr. Buell's brother. Their grandmother had died and left some money."

She saw the spark in Scottie's red-brown eyes. "How much money?" he asked.

"It was left only to a friend," she said coldly. "You'd better go back to sleep."

"For now . . ." he agreed, and she went back to her chair and her book. "I'll kill him," she told herself, no longer frightened by the idea. "I'll have to kill him."

When Toomey returned a half hour later, Connie told her that their patient had roused once. "He gave no trouble."

10

THAT DAY came to an end, and the next was got through—and the next. Scottie was improving, getting better. Surely now he could be moved to a hospital—but he stayed on in the guest room, allowed to eat soft food, allowed to be propped up on pillows. Without checking with Dr. Buell, Toomey would sometimes leave Connie in charge of her patient, but never for very long.

Connie was quite willing to sit in the sickroom.

"You should be my nurse full-time," Scottie told her. "That way you could put arsenic in my boiled egg, or lye in my tea. . . ."

Connie did not answer him

"Of course you want to kill me," Scottie taunted her. "And you could. Though you should have done it when I was out. A pillow over my head would have been the easiest, though wouldn't the autopsy have shown a little broken bone in my throat? I believe suffocated or strangled people do show that. They struggle, you see, and—"

"Stop it!" cried Connie.

He shrugged. "I don't blame you for wanting to kill me. You have things nice here, and with me out of the way, there would be no need to share it. In your spot I'd have found a way to eliminate me. Of course, if you're clumsy, and even if you're pretty smart, there would be an inquest. That could mean an indictment, and trial—and an awful lot of things could come out. . . ."

"That's enough talking," said Connie firmly.

"Maybe you should let me talk as much, and get as excited, as I want to—when we're alone, I mean. That way, I might have another attack—"

She said nothing.

"You like that idea, I think. By the way, are you still sleeping with the doctor?"

Connie stared at him, furious and frightened.

He shrugged. "I don't especially care. You must have married him at least five years ago—or thought you did. What's a few nights or so now?"

After that session, Connie decided that she would not again sit with Scottie. She would ask John to move him out of the house.

But she did not mention the matter to John, and the next day she relieved Toomey in the early afternoon. Scottie seemed to be sleeping.

But fifteen minutes after she had taken up her position in the suite's sitting room, he spoke to her without opening his eyes.

"I've decided that you shouldn't try to kill me, Connie."

She looked at him, but did not speak.

He stirred in the bed, and she half rose from the chair. What if he tried to get up?

He did not. He had only shifted his position a little. "The

best thing for you to do," he said, "is for you to let me go quietly away when I am able. . . ."

"Would you do that?" she asked, hope tricking her into response.

"Oh, sure," he said. "There would be some if's of course."

She settled back in her chair.

"Well, sure," he told her. "You can tell I'm in no condition to work at much of a job. I've got to live, and I'd be most interested in living easy. The way I figure it, if I leave you here living in a state of sin with the doctor, *you* should stand ready to fix things up pretty nice for me."

"Blackmail."

"That's right. But I'd keep quiet."

And she knew for how long she could trust him. "I'll have Dr. Buell's brother draw up a contract," she said dryly.

He laughed. "I know you would," he agreed.

It was a line of thought which she had not previously pursued. To tell Birch, to talk to him, relying on his professional obligation to keep her secret. Oh, but that would destroy Birch! And herself! She might as well, she had better talk to John! Which she should have done, that first night, a week ago.

"If I could leave here," Scottie was saying, his tone musing, "and no inquiry made as to who I am, or about what that tall whippersnapper calls my breaking and entering . . ."

"You had no right coming in as you did!" Connie told him.

"Didn't I?" asked Scottie. "Into my *wife*'s home?"

The look on his face was sly, threatening. Connie could not speak, and it was just as well. . . .

"Yes," he said after a pause. "I would leave here—that would be best—and let you stay. And everything could go along the way you like to have them—your home, your car, pretty clothes, your kids, the doctor. All you'd need to do would be to see I got a check regularly. I'll find me a place to live in the city. You could call the money a contribution to charity."

He had it all worked out—everything in his favor. Once more Connie decided that she would not sit with him again, be alone with him. And if she did not?

He would talk. To Toomey, to Emma—to anyone. John. So—she would have to think of something, some way. Time was needed. She could gain that by seeming to be passive.

Talking to her, he would reveal his plans. Surely there must be some way to handle this man, to silence him, and not harm John or the children.

She no longer considered herself. Though to touch him was revolting, and the thought of his touching her made her physically ill, she did face the possibility of going off with him.

But he didn't want that, probably. Not without the money he felt he could get. That first night he would have taken her person—it was in his struggle for her that he had suffered the attack. But now, and for the time to come, she was more valuable to him right where she was, posing as John's wife—

The whole situation was disgusting. It was making Connie ill. She did not sleep, she had headaches, she was short-tempered. She knew that she was, and John, of course, detected her state. If he but guessed that Scottie was still threatening her . . .

A trial for murder, with John the accused, would not help at all!

And not being able to decide what to do, she went along, doing nothing, though she constantly thought about what was happening to her even as she attempted to carry on as usual.

Everything, everything, reminded her of the horror in which she lived. If she watched TV, hoping to relax, even the soap operas betrayed her. Here was a character wanting to know how to get a marriage license. And on the telephone, the actress was met by a recording in the voice of a robot. "To apply for a wedding license, a blood test is needed, and a physical examination by an accredited physician. There will then be a wait of three days. If either party has been married before . . ." Connie stiffened. "Papers showing proof of divorce or death must be brought. . . ."

She slumped back in her chair. Divorce, death—they would expect the "party" to tell of any previous marriage. And of course Connie should have had proof of Scottie's death; the friendly recorder at home should have demanded that proof; she should certainly have told John of that other marriage.

It would have made no difference. He loved her. Had they done things right then, now Scottie would be having his heart attack in some hospital charity ward, and Connie . . .

The story would probably have to come out—publicly. But maybe something could be salvaged. Given a little time, she surely could find a way to hurt the fewest number of people. She even would hope to save something of herself, for herself. Not pride, especially. She could not hope for that. But given time— She did not want any of the Buells to think she had married John in a calculating way, deliberately. She did not want them to think she was worse than Irene!

Oh, if she could only wipe out the past years. As much as she loved and cherished John, her home, her children— If she could be—well—where Carrie Lee Riddle was today. Or even

Sophia, whose "mouth turned down." If she were any young girl, with life and love before her . . .

She was not old, but already Connie had lived the life of an old woman. Experience had piled upon her in heaps and heaps.

Yes, she wished she could be Sophia, or even Carrie Lee. Now there was a strange switch to her thinking, because it did seem that Sophia, the all-but-disinherited, was the lucky one. Beeze loved her.

John's brothers. Beeze actively was opposed to Scottie's being kept here at the house, or anywhere except in a hospital prison ward. Birch could reason about the situation, and be more detached. He considered John's vulnerability as a doctor.

Connie thought both brothers-in-law liked her, and that they were, to a degree, fond of her. They sensed that she was disturbed by what had happened—as what woman would not be? they probably reasoned. But they seemed aware, too, of John's concern, over and above the concern a doctor gives to a case.

Did John—had John—talked to his brothers? About the extra concern he was feeling? About his worries as they involved Connie, his wife?

Birch talked to John about Irene.

And probably John did talk to Birch.

That afternoon, Mrs. Toomey stayed away a little longer than usual. She had gone to the beauty parlor, and bad luck caused Beeze to drop in while Connie was still sitting with the sick man in the guest suite. She heard him talking to the children, who were in the pool, and she hoped he would accept their shouted invitation to join them. He kept trunks and other personal things in one of the upper-level guest rooms.

But these were not Connie's days. He asked for Connie and came down to the terrace only five minutes ahead of Toomey, but it was long enough.

Discovering what she was doing, he strode into Scottie's room and told Connie she could "go upstairs."

"I'll sit with your guest," he announced.

Of course he could not. Of course Connie did not want him to do that. And of course Beeze did not pay one bit of attention to her efforts to send him away. Even after Toomey returned, he sat on and talked to Scottie. He talked about baseball, and the upcoming election. He asked Scottie what he did for a living. . . .

He suggested that the sick man would soon be well enough to get out of bed. And, if he didn't move on to a hospital, he could, with a wheelchair, sit out on the terrace. Beeze thought he knew where he could borrow a wheelchair. . . .

He made himself a shield between Scottie and Connie, and, finally, almost in tears, she begged him to leave.

She was clumsy about the whole thing. If she hadn't made such a point of his going, he would not have become so troubled about her, and he would have left when Toomey came in. He would not have said anything to John—who literally raised the roof to know that Connie had been sitting with "Bill Scott." That was when Connie first knew the name Scottie was using in her home.

John laced Toomey out, and he was stern with his wife.

"As a nurse, dear . . ." she attempted to justify herself and Mrs. Toomey.

"If Mrs. Toomey needed relief, a word to me would have arranged things. Surely caring for one man, not too sick, couldn't be so very difficult. She knew this was twenty-four-hour duty. . . ."

Connie expected the nurse to walk off the case. She did not. And Connie took her first chance to apologize for John's anger. "Dr. Buell's brother made all the trouble," she said.

Mrs. Toomey nodded. "I understand," she said. "He thinks Mr. Scott should be out of bed and out of the house."

"Is he able?"

"Oh, sure. I won't be on this case but for a few more days."

"You do need relief."

"I'll manage. I just hope the doctor ain't mad at you."

Connie smiled at the big woman. "If he is, he probably has cause."

"You're so right!" said Mrs. Toomey heartily. Connie decided not to ask her what she meant.

A few days later Scottie was wheeled out to the sunshine on the terrace. He looked very white—sicker, Connie thought, than he had looked in bed. Maybe he wouldn't have the strength . . .

She busied herself with some telephone calls which she should have made days and days ago. And only gradually did she become aware that the children's voices were coming from downstairs instead of from their playroom or the front lawn.

She went out on the deck and leaned over the rail. Yes. There was Grey, carrying one of the cats, and Corey huffing and puffing along, trying to keep up, and trying to carry the other cat, who was most unhappy. She heard Scottie's voice—Grey answered him.

"Sure they scratch," he said. "Corey isn't big enough to hold a cat right."

This always infuriated his sister, to be reminded of her lack of seniority, so she screamed at Grey; the cat struggled free, squawling, and bounded down the slope, his dark tail curled high with indignation. Connie's descent on the little domestic gathering added nothing to the gaiety or serenity.

Where had Madie got to? she demanded. She was supposed . . .

The children had been told not to go on the terrace while the sick man was there. . . .

They'd been told not to pick up the cats, too!

"The man doesn't look sick," Grey told his mother.

"Well, he is sick," said Connie sharply.

Scottie sat and watched the scene, smiling. Connie was upset, frightened. And the children were puzzled. They never before had been told to shun people, certainly not those who came to their home.

"I talk to the pump man," Grey reminded her logically.

Connie realized that her fright had shattered her self-control. "This is different," she said, reaching for Corey's hand.

"He isn't a strange man in an automobile," Grey pointed out.

"Oh, don't argue with me!" cried poor Connie.

Corey was going along with her mother, but Grey hung back. "I want to see the roller chair," he said stubbornly. He advanced toward Scottie. "I'm Grey Buell," he said. "What's your name?"

Connie was ready to scream—to snatch the children, to put them inside, and then push Scottie—and his roller chair—down the hill! Anything to get him away and protect her children!

Scottie was watching her, and his smile broadened when she came close enough to snatch at Grey's arm and drag him away by force. Mrs. Toomey came outside to see what was going on, and Madie came flying around the corner. By then, Grey was shrieking and fighting Connie's strong hold on his wrist.

"You're hurting me!" he cried. "I don't think—mothers—are supposed to hurt their children!"

"The kid's right, you know," calmly said Scottie's voice behind them.

Connie handed the children over to Madie.

"I had to change my pinafore, ma'am," said the nursemaid. "I spilled grape juice on it."

Connie brushed her hair back from her face. "I don't want them down here on the terrace," she said wearily. "For a time."

"No, ma'am. I understand."

Contritely, Connie watched the children and Madie go around the corner of the house.

Mrs. Toomey tactfully withdrew.

"I'll bet she does understand," drawled Scottie.

Connie whirled on him, her face still flushed, her eyes angry—and frightened.

"And the kid's right, too," he continued. "You aren't supposed to hurt your children."

"I don't want them down here," Connie said hoarsely. "With *you!*"

"That's what we all understand," Scottie agreed. "Because you are making us understand. You sure are giving yourself away, my dear."

Connie moved toward the stairs. She would go up, gather some calm and repose, and then try to find a way to reinstate herself with Grey and Corey, with Madie. . . .

"It would be much, much better," Scottie said, still in that cool, logical voice, "if you would let me leave."

On his terms, he meant. But, yes, that would be better. Anything would be better!

"Then why don't you go?" Connie cried tensely. "As soon as possible!"

Scottie nodded. "Well, I'll need a few things—we'd have to make some arrangements. . . ."

Almost blindly, Connie stumbled up the stairs, away from him.

She spent the afternoon with the children; she took them out in the car, stopping at the puppet show at the Art Museum, and letting them go along with her when she shopped at the supermarket—a rare treat, indeed.

Grey probably was old enough to guess that he was being bribed. But he did love his pretty young mother, and men in roller chairs were not nearly so important as puppets with red hair and green skin, and a big, big cold white box simply *full* of ice cream bars!

It was about those things that he told his father that evening.

"Popsickles!" Corey displayed her new word.

John laughed and looked at Connie. "You seem to have had quite a day."

"We did," she said, not smiling.

That night she wept in her sleep, quietly, desolately, not rousing to consciousness. John heard her and touched her wet cheeks with the tips of his fingers. Then he slipped out of bed, drew the curtains, and stood with his hands raised, away from his body, the palms turned inward. He gazed at the moonlight, at the clouds . . . and the shadows.

11

THE NEXT morning Connie was tired, drained, and resigned to the nightmare which had come into her life, and which must end. John and the children should not, and must not, suffer from its horror. She no longer mattered. There obviously was no escape for her. But she could free her home and her family from this menace.

It was Saturday morning; John had gone to the hospital, but only for rounds. He would be at home most of that day, and of course on Sunday.

But on Monday, Connie would herself take Scottie away. She would put him in a hospital, or a nursing home— She would find a place! She would pay for his care. . . .

Then she would tell John what she had done, and why. And *then* she would leave.

That was her plan, and she would see it through. The week end survived, she would do what must be done.

That morning she moved about the house, looking pale. "I have a headache," she explained to solicitous Madie. John came home in time to eat lunch with her and the children; he wanted to play golf. No, Connie would not play with him, but she would go to the club. Grey immediately set up a clamor. Connie agreed that she would take the children. They could play with their friends in the pool or on the swings.

"Miss their naps and go to bed early," John predicted.

"Miss their naps and be cross," Connie agreed.

But that was how they spent their afternoon, a handsome young family, the tall doctor in blue Bermudas, white shirt, and ancient white cap. Connie in a shift of pink linen, the children dressed alike in gleaming white.

They all came home tired; the children were bathed, and Corey fell asleep over her supper. John and Connie ate on the upper deck by the light of candles in hurricane lamps, and were about as sleepy as the children.

"We're getting old," John told his wife. "In bed by ten o'clock on Saturday night."

Sunday was more difficult. Church took care of the morning, but they had company all afternoon. And it rained.

Having been sitting on the terrace, the group moved to the lower-level playroom, and "Bill Scott" moved in with them. Birch and Irene were there, and Beeze showed up at three with Sophia Riddle.

"Shouldn't Mr. Scott be resting?" Connie managed to ask Mrs. Toomey, who was watching TV in the sitting room of the guest suite.

"Did Doctor say for me to fetch him?"

No, "Doctor" had not said so. He was watching Scottie, a half smile on his face. The stranger was being extravagantly gallant to Miss Riddle, and the girl was flattered.

She was a very nice girl, though not a pretty one. She was thrilled that Beeze Buell had singled her out. Most attractive men preferred her sister. She was thrilled to be brought, in this way, to meet Beeze's family. Well, actually, she knew them, but there was something rather formal in this presentation.

"Maybe we should move up to the living room," Connie suggested.

"The rain won't last," John assured her. "We can go outside again when it's over."

He was probably right. This seemed to be only a summer shower.

Connie listened to Scottie talking to Sophia. Of course the girl had thought she must pay some attention to the guest of the Buells, a man in a wheelchair. He said he had suffered a heart attack. . . . "And now you come in, and my pulse is racing again."

"Bro-ther!" Connie heard Beeze say disgustedly.

But Sophia seemed to be liking that sort of thing. She blushed, she smiled, and Scottie redoubled his efforts; he even took the girl's hand and patted it.

He was wearing a robe of John's over his pajamas. Two weeks of Toomey's baths had cleaned him up; his hair was a bit long, but not out of fashion for those days. And Scottie had always known how to attract the girls.

Was he being serious? Wryly, Connie thought that here might be her chance. She remembered that Scottie had overheard their talk about the Riddle inheritance. Should she tell him he had the wrong girl? Though ten thousand would sound comfortably large to Scottie.

He— She stiffened. What was he holding in his hand? Showing it to Sophia, talking about the fragile cup as if he owned it, as if *he* had brought it to Connie from France. . . .

Why, that cup— She kept it on the big coffee table up in

the living room. John had brought it to her from a trip he had made when Corey was only three weeks old, and Connie could not go with him. She treasured that cup! For its beauty, for its lovely flower design, its fragility—and because John had carefully brought it home to her. Connie herself always washed it and replaced it on the table upstairs. Upstairs . . .

How had it got down here? The children? No! They would not go into the living room alone, and they would not have brought a cup and saucer down the stairs. The servants were well aware of what that cup meant to Mrs. Buell.

Scottie! Scottie had been upstairs! He had, left on the terrace yesterday afternoon, or perhaps this morning—he had wheeled his chair around to the front of the house, or he could have walked. Beeze thought the man was "soldiering" —that he was stronger than he let on. And he probably was.

Because he had to have been up in the living room. Where else had he poked and pried? Touching Connie's things, daring to—

She walked across the room and held out her hand for the cup, too angry to think clearly about what she was doing.

Scottie looked up at her and held the cup away from her reach.

"Give it to me!" she said tensely. She went around his chair, and he threw his hand forward, again out of her reach —and the cup slipped from his fingers, crashed against the far wall.

"*Whoops!*" said Scottie, grinning at Sophia.

Connie, her lips thin, went over and stooped to pick up the pieces of china.

John came to help her. "I'm sorry, my dear. I thought you kept that upstairs."

She did not look at him. Her dark hair falling forward

across her face, she picked up each shred and shard. She did not want John to see her tears, and certainly not Scottie. She carefully retrieved every scrap, and, watching her, John's face was torn with pity for her. Poor girl. These days she was not adding to her treasures. Rather, she seemed to be taking and spending what she had had in store. John felt this, and he thought Connie knew, as well, what was happening to her hoard.

"I'm sorry," said Sophia Riddle behind them. "Was it something special?"

Connie stood up, found the saucer, and put her tinkling heap of china into it. "Yes," she said. "It was special." She carried the saucer out of the room, not knowing herself what she would do with it. When she left this house, she would abandon so many special things. Still, she could not dump her cup into the trash can. She found a paper bag in the laundry room and put the saucer and china bits into it, then tucked the package away on a shelf.

When she came back along the terrace, she could hear Beeze talking loudly to Scottie. He was a clumsy oaf! he shouted. "Why anyone should touch a thing like that . . . Why, you couldn't even get one of your fat fingers through its handle. You—"

Connie ran the last few steps. Beeze must not! He simply must not. . . .

"I feel I was partly to blame," said poor Sophia unhappily.

"No, you were not!" cried Beeze. "It's this guy. . . ."

Connie touched his arm. "Please, dear . . ." she said softly.

He jerked away from her, walked to the terrace door, and strode out. She followed him. "You must not forget that Mr. Scott has a bad heart," she told him.

Beeze made a growling sound in his throat.

"Please, dear?" Connie said again.

He glared at her. "Do you like that guy?" he asked angrily.

"Oh, no!" she said quickly. "I—"

"You what?"

She sighed. "I—we can't hurt him, Beeze."

He shook his head. "I don't get it," he said. "What has got into you, Connie? What's *wrong* with you?"

"Don't badger her, Beeze," said John's voice behind them. "Connie's been having a difficult time. A sick man in the house for this long . . ."

"Yeah, yeah, yeah," said Beeze. "And *what* a sick man! Don't you think there's some kind of hanky-panky going on around here? Who is this guy anyway? Why did he come to the house in the first place? Why does Connie want you to keep him here?"

"It was my idea to keep him here," said John firmly. "Connie had no voice in the matter."

"She usually has a voice in things concerning her home, doesn't she? All right then. Who is this character in connection with *you?* Why don't *you* get rid of him? I spotted him for a no-good the first minute I saw him. Road bum. But here he is, sitting pretty—"

"And you're jealous because he was pleasant to your girl," said John, his eyes smiling.

Beeze started to deny this, then he grinned sheepishly. "All right," he agreed. "I didn't like that! And I shouldn't think you'd want him to be charming—or *pleasant,* as you say—to your girl either. But you go off, leaving him in your home where Connie is. D'you think that's wise? I find her sitting by his bed. . . ."

"As a nurse," said John, no longer smiling. "You don't want to get into this too deeply, do you?"

"I don't know," cried Beeze unhappily. "I just don't *know!* And what's more, I don't think you know, either."

John walked away from them for a few feet. "I know only one thing," he said, his voice tight and husky. "This thing has hurt Connie, and I am determined to heal that bruise."

Connie gasped. She must— She must—

Blindly she ran to the stairs and stumbled up them. She, too, knew only one thing—that she was going to fight Scottie. She was going to fight any way and anyone necessary to keep John, to keep her children—and her house.

She stayed in her room for fifteen minutes. No one came in search of her, and she gratefully thanked John. She must return to the terrace, she must look and be composed, she—

Her make-up freshened, her hair brushed, she came downstairs to greet new friends who had come to their house. Dr. Bennet, John's assistant, and his nice wife. Fortunately a talkative woman, she would take over any group if let alone.

Saree was a busy person, she did welfare work, she was active in the campaign to preserve landmark buildings, she always had interesting things to talk about. Connie could take up her duties as hostess, managing to touch John's shoulder as she brought him iced tea. . . .

"Tea?" he asked her.

"With our guest-patient," she said composedly, "I thought it was better."

"Maybe you should explain that to Benny?"

"I'll let you do that."

He watched her, nodding, as puzzled by the quick change in her as he had been by her previous "nerves," but not worried. In this mood, he thought, he could talk to her, and—

Meanwhile, Beeze was doing some talking, and Scott was

answering him. Someone had explained to Benny and Saree who Mr. Scott was. That he had become ill while visiting the house. . . .

"But we don't know much about him," said Beeze truculently. "For instance, you've never told us what you do, Mr. Scott."

Scottie smiled and tinkled the ice in his tall glass of tea. "I would have to be *Dr.* Scott," he said slowly.

"Not really," drawled Beeze, meaning exactly what he said.

Scottie smiled at him. "Oh, yes," he said easily. "That was one reason I stopped here the other night. I have this bad heart. I haven't been able to conduct a practice. In fact—" he laughed shortly—"I was on my uppers. I was feeling badly—I knew that Dr. Buell lived here, and I felt sure the profession would stand by me."

"And it did," said Beeze dryly. "Dr. Scott, eh?"

"Yes, sir. Dr. William Scott. Usually called Scottie."

Connie sighed. He usually was called Scottie. And his name, so far as she knew, was William Scott. William Scott Stringer. Beside that, he was lying. He was not, and never had been, a doctor. He had, years and years ago, been a science teacher in a small-town high school. What he had done since, she had no knowledge of, but she would bet that he had not been studying medicine.

She could not, of course, reveal any of her knowledge of him, but she did mean to stop this particular masquerade—and quickly.

George Bennet was talking to Scottie politely, not very interested. He asked where his home was. Chicago? Where had he trained?

To her relief, very soon Scottie announced that he was

tired, and Toomey came to fetch him.

Next day, Connie would talk to the man. The fake, the charlatan. He was even faking his fatigue. He had managed to get upstairs, hadn't he? Though that expedition could have tired him—John would not have been fooled about the actual state of his heart. He was telling Bennet about it, and said that the condition seemed to be a chronic one. She heard emphysema mentioned.

In any case, Scottie disappeared for the rest of the evening. Maybe he was tired.

However, the next morning, she accused him of faking. "Though I happen to know you did do too much yesterday."

Mrs. Toomey was changing the bed. Scottie sat in the wheelchair, and his color was bad.

"Just enough to keep himself sick, not enough to kill him," Connie told herself.

"I was going to ask you, Mrs. Buell," said Toomey, stretching a draw sheet. "Did he have some hard liquor yesterday?"

"Oh, no!" said Connie quickly. "I know he shouldn't drink." Scottie never had been able to hold liquor.

Mrs. Toomey carried her bundle of used linen to the laundry, and Connie followed her. "I been meaning to ask," said the nurse, her voice low. "D'you keep the stuff down here?"

"The stuff?" asked Connie. "Oh, you mean liquor. No. We don't. But he could get it upstairs."

Mrs. Toomey's sandy eyebrows went up.

"He's been upstairs," said Connie firmly.

"Oh, ma'am, he couldn't have!"

"Yes," said Connie. "I think he could. And he'd go again. If there were something he really wanted to do, or get, up there."

Mrs. Toomey snorted. "I watch him pretty close."

"You should," said Connie.

Something Scottie wanted . .

Connie checked on the children, busy in the sandbox. It was Madie's day off, and she was in charge. Grey was busily filling a small pail from the birdbath and taking the water back to whatever building project was in progress. He would be in a mess within minutes, and Corey, too. Well—

What had Scottie wanted upstairs? Gin, probably. Not the cup. He had brought that down on impulse. Perhaps that first night she had by some gesture or word indicated that it was a treasure. He would know how to upset her. . . .

How long had he been upstairs? How much searching had he done? Had he hunted for money? Connie's pulse jumped. Was he planning to leave? To walk out?

If so, Connie would help him. Oh, indeed she would help him!

She hurried her steps back to the terrace. She sat down on the couch-swing, not looking directly at Scottie, who had moved to the long chair. It offended Connie to see him there. That was John's favorite chair in which to sit, and sun, and rest.

"Scottie," she said quietly.

"Shouldn't you be careful, using that name?" he asked.

"You told quite a few people yesterday that you were called Scottie. That was when you were also saying that you were a doctor, and that you were tired. Both fakes, of course."

"Oh?"

"Certainly. As I know."

"I was tired. I'm still tired."

"Perhaps you did too much, going upstairs."

"Now see here, Connie!" He raised his head so that he

could scowl at her.

She kept her serenity. "Shouldn't *you* be careful?" she asked. "And I've already told Toomey that you went upstairs. But there is something I'll have to tell you, Scottie Stringer. Don't you try doing anything that will touch my husband's profession. Don't you do it!"

"Your husband," he said reflectively.

"Yes. Legally or not, common-law—whatever—he is my husband, and he comes first in the world to me. So I am warning you—"

"It could be that his profession is the thing that comes first in the world with him. Did you mean that?"

"It does come first."

Scottie smiled. "Ahead of you?"

"Certainly. Ahead of anything."

"And that's all right?"

"Well, of course it's all right."

"Women!" he said, shaking his head.

Mrs. Toomey came out on the terrace, glanced at them, then she walked down to where she could see the children and talk to them. Their clear young voices rang like glass bells in the sunshine. Connie thought wistfully of the time, only days behind her, when she could have played happily with her children, or sat near them, watchful, with her book, her sewing, her—

"I had hoped," she said to Scottie, "forgetting that this would be Madie's day off, and that I had made no arrangements with a sitter—I had hoped to move you today to a nursing home. But we can do that tomorrow."

Scottie said nothing.

"You're able," said Connie.

"I won't go." He did not open his eyes.

"Oh, now, look."

"I won't go!" he said sharply. "And if you know what's best for you, you won't try to make me go."

"Have you any thought you can stay on here indefinitely?"

"We'll work something out," he told her. "Until we do, don't make the fuss it will cause if you try to move me out of here against my will." His face, his small, mean eyes told that he meant what he said. He would make a fuss.

Connie bit her lip to keep still, to keep from lashing out at him, from screaming to him all the things she wanted to say to this man and about him. Her fear, her dread, had built up in her until if she would ever let go—

She thought wistfully of her reasonable little plan. The nursing home—she was on the Board, and when, that morning, she had called, the manager had said he would "find a place" for Mr. Scott. He would be happy to accommodate Dr. and Mrs. Buell. It had seemed a plan so simple as to be entirely possible. Except for Scottie . . .

"Mommy, look! Mommy, *look!*"

Startled, Connie jumped, knocking an ash tray from the table beside her. And she managed to find a smile for Grey, who was bringing his "cake" to show her. It was a birthday cake, he assured her. He held the round mass of wet sand carefully on the small shovel. Its "candle" was listing badly. She straightened the small stick.

"It's a beautiful cake," she told her son.

"Chocklick!" announced Corey. Her fat bare feet curled on the terrace stones with happiness in this achievement.

"But we can't eat it," Grey reminded her.

"No, no!" said the little girl.

"Let me see it," called Scottie. "I especially like chocolate cake."

Connie would have protested—but that other day—"Show the gentleman your cake," she told the little boy. "Then we'll get some dry shorts."

His denim shorts, his striped t-shirt, were soaked and smeared with wet sand.

Corey followed her brother and, knowing no fear of people, she crawled up on the footrest of the chaise, the better to look at Grey's confection. Scottie was helping Grey hold the shovel, and he was talking to both children—charmingly. Connie knew how charmingly he could talk.

He was discussing cakes with the children as gravely as a scientist would discuss the components of a nuclear bomb with his colleagues.

"I believe it's a matter of too much water," Scottie told Grey. "You diluted your solids. D'you know what *dilute* is?"

Corey steadied herself with a pudgy hand on Scottie's arm, and she stood up precariously, the better to see the cake. "I like salad," she said solemnly, and Grey laughed merrily at his sister. He explained the joke to Scottie, who laughed, too.

"If you hadn't got so much of *your* solids on yourself," Scottie told the boy, "your cake would hold up better."

Connie could not bear to have Corey's small, soft hand touch that man, she was terrified of Scottie's hand upon Grey's. He should not be privileged to know this intimacy with her children!

He seemed genuinely interested in those children, though, she had learned, nothing was genuine with Scottie Stringer. Connie went across the stones. "Let's put the cake back in the sandbox," she said. She lifted Corey down from the chair. "Come along, Grey."

He obeyed, though reluctantly. His sand confections were not often so well received.

"Put your things away, and then we'll get cleaned up," Connie told the children. She watched them make their way along the terrace and across the grass. The cake collapsed entirely before they reached the box, and the children laughed happily.

"Gather the sand up in your pail," Connie called, "but don't dig into the grass."

Then she turned on Scottie. "I don't want you to touch or talk to the children again!" she said tightly. "Do you understand me?"

"Sure I understand you." He stretched out on the chaise, crossing his legs. "What's more, those smart kids can understand you pretty quick, too."

"Just remember what I say," Connie told him. "For the short time you're here."

In a second, he was on his feet. He had his hand on her shoulder, he bent over her, his face red, his eyes glittering. "Let's name a few things for you to remember!" he cried loudly. "You don't tell me what I can and can't do, understand?" He gave Connie a shake—her dark hair flew, and she struggled to get free of him.

"You're damn hoity-toity about those kids!" Scottie was shouting. "You're damn hoity-toity about yourself! Don't touch this, don't touch that! You—"

"Mr. Scott!" It was Toomey, coming up with the wheelchair.

The children had raced back to the terrace.

"Let go my mommy!" cried Grey, kicking at Scottie.

"She's crying! You hurt her!"

It was a terrible scene. It promised to get worse. Connie struggled against Scottie's grasp, wanting to console her frightened children, to protect them. They were crying, terribly.

And the chow dog . . .

He came charging, and he must not. All they needed was for Scottie to have a dog bite. . . . Scottie drew back, both hands up to his face.

Connie was free. "Sit, Yang!" she screamed at the dog. "Sit! "

Yes, it was a terrible scene, the children screaming, the dog barking furiously.

Cleve came running. And of course it took a man to handle a thing of that sort.

"How we must have looked!" Connie told herself, gathering Corey's streaked face comfortingly to her shoulder, reaching for Grey's hand. "We'll go upstairs," she said in a muffled tone.

Cleve and Toomey had put Scottie into the wheelchair and were taking him to the guest suite. Connie thought Toomey said something about that man having to quiet down.

What had been *done?* What had been *said?* Connie tried to remember. She took the children upstairs, stripped their dirty clothes away, and washed them. They indignantly refused to consider a bath. She would keep them up here, or take them away from the house in the car. Tomorrow she would arrange things with John. Scottie would leave. Connie would enlist Toomey's help. It must be clear to her that the man was dangerous.

"Are you all right, madame?"

It was Cleve, standing solicitously in the living room doorway. Connie had the children at the game table in the sacrosanct place. They were pushing dominoes about. Her eyes misted as she looked up at this kind man. This gentleman! Twenty years older than she was, perhaps thirty, concerned only for his mistress, whom he respected, to whom he owed care and protection.

"I'm all right, Cleve," she said softly.

"Yes, ma'am. Mrs. Toomey has given Mr. Scott a sedative."

Connie sighed and nodded. "He'll sleep then," she said. "The children and I will stay where we won't disturb him."

"Yes, ma'am." Cleve stood, still uncertain, in the doorway.

"Don't worry," Connie told the man. "This is an—an unfortunate situation. And I hope you will not speak to Dr. Buell about what happened. Since Mr. Scott is leaving soon, there should be no more trouble."

"Yes, ma'am." The houseman turned back to look at her. "When Mrs. Toomey said that—I was helping her get Mr. Scott to bed—when she said he would be leaving, he laughed, madame."

Connie nodded. "I know," she agreed.

12

Connie let the children "help" fix lunch, an unusually messy performance, but it made them so happy, and took so much time, that they were ready for their naps without much argument. She then busied herself in her bedroom, selecting garments that should go to the cleaner; she would take them if the children woke in time for a drive. She attended to her person, and carefully selected a dress to wear, though she would not put it on until Grey and Corey were dressed and ready.

They managed their expedition away from the house. Connie took the children to see friends out in the country who had little chickens to watch and feed.

Corey almost exploded trying to tell her father about it when he came home that evening—early. He glanced over his shoulder at Connie in her short, slim white dress. "What on earth did they *see?*" he asked.

"Yellow baby chicks. She's telling you."

Grey was showing how they scratched, and Corey tried to mock him, which caused her to tumble into a heap. John scooped her up and held her high, laughing and kicking.

Connie watched the tall man, clean-cut, laughing as he played with his children, turning now and then to send his honest, good smile to their mother. In contrast, to think of the grubby scene which those children had witnessed eight hours before. . . .

"I brought you something," John told her.

"A present?" asked Grey.

"Not for you, young man. For Mommy."

"Let me see it anyway," the boy suggested.

John chuckled and looked around for his suit jacket. "I had a coat, didn't I?" he asked.

"I hung it away," Connie told him, going to fetch it.

The children pushed between them, and were obviously disappointed to see the small paper sack which he drew out of his side pocket.

"Woolworth's," said John, as if he were announcing a gift from Tiffany's.

"All for me?" asked Connie, making a valiant try to play his game.

John carefully unwrapped tissue paper. " Easy does it," he cautioned Grey. "We mustn't break this. Here, Mommy! All for you! "

Connie could not speak. All she could do was to hold the little cup and saucer in her two hands. Of white china, gold-rimmed, it was not even a pretty cup, but—

"He . . . " she gasped. "He . . . "

"Yes," said John. "He did. And we'll talk about that later. Now! Do we eat with the kids?"

"It's Monday."

"So it is. I look forward to it all week."

Connie laughed, wrapping the cup again in its tissue paper, then unwrapping it. "Thank you, John," she said shyly.

"It's an earnest. When I can find a week free, I'll take you to France, in person, to buy a good one."

"I like this."

She took the cup inside to place on the coffee table; she told Emma that they would eat supper whenever it was ready.

"Shouldn't I broil a steak for the doctor, ma'am?"

"Did you make his hamburger special?"

"Oh, yes, ma'am."

"He'll eat that. He likes your good hamburger."

"Yes, ma'am. And Grey won't make a fuss."

"As he would over a steak," agreed Connie.

They ate dinner, which went more tidily than it sometimes did. Corey demanded a napkin instead of a bib, but their worst fears were not realized. John said it was his turn to give the baths. "You'll drown," Connie predicted.

"Where's my rubber apron?"

The baths were fun, but the story hour was interrupted by Grey's announcement that he'd forgot, but he had something secret to tell Daddy.

"Oh, dear," sighed Connie. Grey's secrets could be complicated.

"I'll read the story first," John said firmly. "When you are tucked in, you can tell me."

"In my room?

"In your room, but with the door open."

This was done. Connie tucked Corey in. John tumbled his son into his bed, and turned down the lamp. "Now," Connie heard him say, "let's have that secret."

John was smart. If he had forgotten, Grey would have made it a means for calling him back.

Grey took a little time to get started, but after several attempts the words came tumbling out, and again terror threatened to rise in their peaceful home. " . . . don't let that man hit Mommy!" she heard the boy cry. "You— Don't let him hit her, Daddy!"

John's voice rumbled reassuringly. He managed to ask if anyone had hit Mommy. What man? Was she hurt? She didn't look hurt. . . . Oh, yes. He, and Grey, must take care of Mommy.

"Now, if you'll go straight to sleep, I'll tell the man that he mustn't do that again."

"I'll shut my eyes and be quiet," the little boy promised.

John came out, his face stern. "I'm going down to see Scott," he told his wife.

"John . . ."

"This won't take long."

He went out through the balcony doors, striding along the deck past the windows. Connie followed him fearfully.

She went no further than the terrace door of the guest suite. Scottie was still in bed, though propped up on pillows. John questioned Mrs. Toomey and read the chart, the light from its page reflected upward into his face.

Scottie watched him, his face sullen.

"I see you had to have a sedative," John said, giving the chart back to the nurse.

"Her idea, not mine."

John picked up the man's wrist. "You didn't overdo? Get excited?"

"You wouldn't believe a thing I said."

"Try me."

"That redheaded broad puts down what she wants. I don't know why you keep her around."

"I thought you needed her."

"I don't need her now."

John sat down in the chair beside the bed. "I think you may be right," he said.

"What do you mean by that?" asked Scottie suspiciously.

John crossed his knees and shook out the slight drape of his blue trouser leg. "Only that I believe the time has come for you to leave here. I am sure you can, safely, now. Perhaps you should stop at the hospital for a check . . ."

Connie saw ugliness building up in Scottie. He would burst out into all sorts of charges and threats. He—

She came into the bedroom. "John," she said, a little breathless with the panic which threatened to engulf her. "I think maybe we should talk about that later. Mr. Scott has had a bad day—" Her voice trembled and broke.

John looked at her curiously.

"Why are you so upset?" he asked, his tone cold.

"Well—" She twisted and braided her fingers together.

"Well," she tried again. "I'll grant that he shouldn't have been kept here. But we did keep him, and now we shouldn't —you know . . . ?"

John stood up, tall and angry. "I hope you are not suggesting that I would abandon a case?" His cold tone had become icy.

Connie stared at him, wide-eyed and alarmed. She prayed that Scottie did not know the legal value of the term. She was shocked. Not at John's anger. She must get used to the idea that he could be angry with her. But she was shocked that he could think she would doubt his professional behavior. Though she must consider that, and he should.

"He can be moved," John said. "He is able to be up, to walk a little. . . . We never did have any obligation to him."

"No," said Connie. "But he is here. A patient. We must

consider him as that, not as a guest who, perhaps, has outstayed his welcome."

"That's nonsense, and you know it!" John cried angrily. He *was* angry. Scottie watched him, and he watched Connie, too—as pleased as Punch. Connie had told him he was leaving. Mrs. Toomey had. The doctor made it official. But now, here was Connie— It would seem that he had gotten to her. Something he had said or done was right—for him.

He raised himself on his pillows. His eyes still showed the sedative which Toomey had given him. "I think the lady's right," he said silkily. "I do seem to need a little more time. Of course I'll try not to make any trouble."

John clapped his hands together. "See that you remember that promise," he told the man roughly. "Mrs. Toomey is here to help you. Do what she tells you to do. The servants and Mrs. Buell are not to be involved."

At John's mention of her name and title, Connie saw Scottie's red-brown eyes narrow. Why didn't he speak out? Why was he waiting?

John gave a few crisp orders to the nurse, he said a few more things to Scottie, then he went upstairs. Connie already was up there, waiting for him.

"I'm sorry, darling," she said to him at once. "But I am afraid that man would make trouble for us, if given a chance."

John nodded wearily. "Let's forget him, shall we?"

"I'll be glad to," said Connie firmly.

"Look— Did he strike you today?"

"No. He talked a little rough. Mrs. Toomey thought he was doing too much. I agreed with her. And—he talked rough. Grey got excited."

"I hope that's all," John said, stretching out on the couch.

"But as I say, let's forget it."

She put records on the player, she stroked his hair as she passed him. He caught at her hand. "Is he smart enough to know about abandonment? " he asked. "Birch mentioned that to me, too, you know. He said I was a fool to keep the guy here at all. But since I had . . ."

Connie didn't need to answer his question. She thought she knew how smart Scottie was, how devious, cunning, ruthless . . .

She hoped John need never find out. She felt toward him as she would toward Grey, or Corey, not wanting him to see or know about the ugliness of Scottie Stringer's world.

During the night, a wind rose, and a hard rain pelted the windows. Connie had forgotten to close the bedroom draperies, and when the telephone rang at six forty-five, listening, she could gaze out upon a world of trees and grass, the sun shining through a light haze. "It looks like green scum," she told herself.

She glanced at John. He was listening to Miss Danford, his hair rumpled down over his forehead. "Hi," his lips said soundlessly to Connie. She smiled at him and sat on the side of the bed, her foot seeking her slipper.

She could faintly hear Miss Danford's voice through the telephone. John would do a pneumothorax—he had a class—and—and— "I will bring your plane tickets with me."

Connie clapped her fingers over her mouth. Oh, dear! She had completely forgotten that trip! She hadn't packed John's bag. . . . She—she broke off, to listen.

Behind her John was saying, "Miss D., I am not going to Atlantic City. Yes, I know there is a meeting of the College of Surgeons."

Connie scrambled to get into her robe.

"Yes," John said patiently. "I did plan to attend. But now I want you to cancel those plans. To cancel everything."

Miss Danford was stammering. John smiled and actually winked at Connie. The collar of his pajama coat was up behind his ears.

"So I'll have some free time!" he said to the nurse. "That's good, Miss D. That is very good. How long was I going to be away? Oh, wonderful. I'll use it right here at home, but you are to forget I said that to you."

Connie went into the bathroom. John was saying, "No, Miss D. I can't leave now. I won't leave. . . ."

When had he decided? Last night, probably. Because of Scottie and what Grey had said to him. Or he would have mentioned his trip to Connie during the evening, to remind her of the packing.

Oh, she was glad he would be at home! Whatever happened—whatever Scottie said, or did, he would be there.

She scooped cold water into her hands, and bathed her face, looking up into the mirror with her black-lashed, gray-blue eyes. They were very wide and round, like Grey's eyes when he was alarmed at something. What if John had been away, in Atlantic City, or someplace, when Scottie first had come to the house? What if—now—

She dried her face and her hands; she ran a comb through her hair. She went swiftly to the children's rooms; they were sleeping soundly. She closed their doors and went on to the kitchen. Orange juice, cold, delicious. Coffee . . .

By the time John had showered, shaved, and begun to dress, she was back with her little tray. He flipped a pink ribbon at the throat of her robe. "Did you hear?" he said. "No work, no hospital, no nuthin' for three glorious days? From noon today until Thursday evening— Boy, am I going to be lazy!"

He drained the glass and reached for his shirt. "Tomorrow," he said, "I'll get up at eight. . . ."

He would not. He would wake at six forty-five and be out of bed by seven.

"And I'll want a proper breakfast. An enormous breakfast."

Connie smiled at him and handed him his striped tie.

"Every morning," he told her. "Two mornings. Let's see." He tilted his chin. "Fried apples one morning. Cut thick, with the peel on. Bran muffins with guava jelly. Or, maybe, that bitter marmalade you get. Blueberry pancakes. Country ham with redeye gravy and biscuits." He stepped into his trousers and reached for the coffee mug. "And be sure I get scrambled eggs with minced clams. I love that mess."

Connie laughed helplessly. "I'll be glad to have you at home," she said when she kissed him.

He departed in his usual burst of speed around the drive and out to the highway. Connie heard Madie come in; she could go back to bed. She did not. She dressed slowly and, taking her small tray with her, she went to the kitchen. She spoke to Emma, and to Madie when she came into the room. Had she had a good day of freedom?

"Oh, yes, ma'am. Were the children good?"

"We did fine. Can I help you?"

"If you can persuade Corey she'll have to have a bath . . . "

"An accident?"

"I'm afraid so. She's only two."

"Of course she is. Maybe she'll want to come into my bathroom."

Madie smiled at her. "Then we'll have Grey unhappy."

"He may come in and watch us when he is dressed."

It was always a privilege for the children to come into their parents' quarters. Connie's pretty bathroom enchanted them. The silver, swan-shaped faucets, the tub into which one stepped down, the pretty towels folded on the glass shelves. There were growing plants before the big window, and this morning Connie could point out a tiny lemon which had appeared on a small, potted tree. Grey must not touch it, but he could stand entranced and peer between the glossy leaves.

Connie put perfumed salts into the warm water, and Madie brought Corey in, wrapped in a blanket. "I didn't do it," the child said of her accident.

"It happened while you were asleep," Connie agreed, sitting on the side of the tub. "We'll manage fine, Madie. Thank you."

"Yes, ma'am. Can I fix your breakfast?"

"Yes. If you will, please. Not too much."

Bathing her baby girl, looking into her upraised, lovely, innocent face, touching her soft body, not for the first time Connie thought about the way she would feel, fourteen years from now, if this exquisite creature would give herself to a boy—a man—like Scottie Stringer.

She trembled with a spasm of grief, loss, and hurt, just to imagine such a thing, feeling a pain worse than she herself had known during that awful, awful time.

The next three days went swiftly. It was incredibly wonderful to have John at home. He dug flower beds and swam in the pool with the children, played croquet with Connie and his brothers. . .

Their friends learned that he was at home only if they happened to come to the house. And they were asked not to spread the word. "He needs this break."

Beeze guessed why John had not gone to Atlantic City, and so did Birch. "That fella's bad medicine," they told each other.

But they, of course, had their own affairs and preoccupations. John could handle his family, his home, and even his guest.

Birch had Irene on his hands. . . .

She herself came up to the house on the first evening of John's vacation, though she was not surprised to find him there at dinnertime. She had walked up the hill. She accepted the cup of coffee which Connie offered her, looked around to determine Cleve's whereabouts, and blurted out that she had decided to divorce Birch. "I know you'll be relieved."

John put his napkin down beside his plate. "Irene . . ." he said helplessly.

"I was not right for him," she said calmly. "You've always known that."

"I consider my opinion unimportant." Connie admired his composure.

Irene lit a cigarette and looked around for a tray. "I know you don't approve of ashes in your good china . . ."

Connie fetched a tray. "I'm sorry if you're unhappy, Irene," she said, not really knowing what to say.

Irene shrugged. "Oh, happiness doesn't much enter into it, Connie," she said. "But I have decided to give the good guy a break."

"Birch, you mean," said John, his voice deep.

"Well, sure I mean Birch." For all her poise, her hardness really, Irene did look unhappy.

"Are you going to marry—someone else?" Connie blurted.

Irene laughed. "If you mean Cliff Adams, no, dear, I am

not. I couldn't do that."

There was a silence. One could hear the children chattering at the far end of the house. Mrs. Toomey had the downstairs TV on. But at the dining-room table there was a long silence. Connie plucked a nasturtium from the green bowl of bright flowers; the candle flames flickered in a small breeze.

"What," John asked, "what does Birch feel about all this?"

Irene shrugged. "He's against divorce in itself," she agreed. "I suppose all the Buells are against it."

"We're a conservative lot," John acknowledged.

"Six weeks ago," Irene said in almost a musing tone, "he asked me for a divorce, you know."

"I knew that he did. But—what does he say about your agreeing? Does he know you don't plan to marry Adams?"

"I told him."

"And what did he say?"

"Oh—" She laughed shortly, dryly, and shook her head. "He said—that guy actually asked me why I didn't try again with him."

She glanced at Connie and at John. She leaned forward. "Do you think I should?" she asked. "Right now I'm thinking of him, you know."

"I see you are. And trying could do no harm."

"No, I suppose not."

She stayed for another fifteen minutes, going with them into the living room, moving restlessly about. She picked up the dime-store cup from the coffee table, raised her eyebrows, set it down. Connie offered no explanation. She thought Irene was trying to say something else, but if so, she didn't get it said. Finally, she departed, going out through the front door and walking down the drive instead of cutting down and back across the lawn.

"Do you think it will work out, John?" Connie asked her husband.

"Probably. She's doing the right thing."

Leaving her seated on the couch with the evening newspaper, he went out to the balcony and down the stairs—to check on Scottie, to talk to the man for a short time. When at home, he did this at regular intervals. He would do it during the next couple of days.

As for Beeze, he, too, was preoccupied with his own affairs. Late the next afternoon, he came to the house, found the family all in the pool, said he did not have time to undress and swim— Could he dangle his feet?

This he did, looking ridiculous in his shirt and tie, the legs of his trousers pulled up to his knees.

"You don't look any older than Corey," he told Connie. "Is John being good to his child bride?"

"What's your big rush?" John asked, lifting himself to sit on the pool edge beside his brother.

"Going to be in a rush for the next six weeks. You still got your freeloader?" He jerked his head down toward the guest room.

"For a short time longer. What's your rush going to be about?"

Beeze looked as if he would pursue the matter of Scottie. Then his excitement took over. "You'll be the first to know," he said. "I'm going to get married!"

"Oh, Beeze!" cried Connie. "Sophia?"

"Well, sure Sophia."

"You said you couldn't afford to."

"I say an awful lot of stuff, Connie. Don't I, John?"

"The heap is overwhelming."

Beeze grinned. "We decided that the ten thousand was big enough that I wouldn't seem to be sorry for her. We don't want to be rich anyway, and now her mouth turns up all the time! "

"It's just wonderful, Beeze," Connie told him. "Wait, I'll get out and kiss you."

"Bring a towel," he called to her. "You'll drip and ruin my make-up."

She brought the towel, and she kissed him. "Tell us your plans," she urged.

"Haven't had time to make many, yet. We'll be married in six weeks—fairly quiet because of Grandma, but John's to be best man, and Sophia said to ask you if you'd be a bridesmaid."

He chattered along, said he hoped they'd get rid of the man who came to dinner in time to help in the celebrations. He talked about where he and Sophia would live. He talked . . .

In six weeks. Connie shivered. Where would she *be* in six weeks? Nobody would want her for a bridesmaid, certainly. And— She went down to the shallow end of the pool and coaxed the children out of the water.

When she came back, dressed, Beeze was gone and, his terry robe bundled about him, John was sitting with Scottie on the terrace. They were talking about emphysema.

John talked to Scottie—or let him talk—about various medical matters. Was he believing the man was a doctor? Could Connie find a way to tell him he was lying?

Scottie talked so much, and she was around only part of the time—though if John was with him, she tried to be about. He was with him often when he was at home.

When he left the terrace, as he did that evening, briefly, to dress, he would quite openly tell Cleve, or the gardener, to keep an eye on Mr. Scott. With Toomey there, and all—

If Scottie knew this and minded—he probably did. But, though he was convalescing rapidly, for the time he seemed not only content, but happy to sit and talk with John endlessly about medicine. He evidently thought he had deceived Dr. Buell.

As she could, Connie listened to them. The men covered a lot of ground in their discussions. They talked about malpractice suits, and Scottie told a lurid tale about a gun-toting doctor he had known. Did Dr. Buell carry a gun? Keep one in the office? His desk?

He told hoary medical jokes as if the subject matter had occurred firsthand with him. "Either sharpen those knives, Nurse, or keep a bottle of tenderizer handy."

Connie had watched John's face during this episode. It told her nothing. She would guess that he was bored.

But she didn't know. She didn't know what was going on at all—what her husband was doing, spending so much time with Scottie. She knew that he did not like the man!

But he was being courteous and even nice to him. He used that same manner talking to acquaintances after church.

Had John snatched his three days of freedom to spend time with Scottie? If so, why?

In the past three weeks, at various times, and certainly now that he was staying at home, Connie had thought—and even been afraid—that John would sit down and talk to her seriously about Scottie.

He had not done this. Would he—ever?

Yes, he would, because she must talk to him. She must—before or after Scottie left—before, and not after, Scottie had told him who he really was.

Had he— The idea struck her like a sharp blow! Had he told John already? Connie shook with sudden terror. If Scottie had told, what sort of game could John be playing? Was he trying to protect her? And himself? Was he trying to catch her? To wait and see if she would tell, what she would tell?

Oh, she could not endure this torture any longer! She hated not being able to trust John more than she had hated any part of the entire horror-filled episode. She hated his not knowing her every thought.

She must find a way to tell John—especially since Scottie had brought this medical deception into the situation. She had warned him not to touch John's profession. Scottie, sometimes, sounded pretty good when he talked about the nursing shortage, the rising costs of hospital building—

But he knew *nothing* about medicine! He was not a doctor! Connie should tell John that he was a fake before he got himself involved with the man. He might even try to find Scottie a job. She felt sure that Scottie himself had some such idea, and was being smugly pleased.

13

Connie set Wednesday night as the time when she would tell John the whole sordid tale. He would be rested, he would still have another day in which to dispose of Scottie and decide what he and Connie would do with their lives. Yes, Wednesday night would be the time.

And of course then, on Wednesday afternoon, there came a frenzied call from Dr. Bennet. His sister's son, a boy of fourteen, had been shot at close range, in the chest. Miss Danford had told Benny where to find John.

Of course John went immediately into the city, to the hospital. He sent back word to Connie that he would not be home for dinner. The situation was grave; he would operate, but—

At midnight he came home, exhausted. The boy was still alive, he said. But what a bloody mess! People who kept guns in their homes, with ammunition available—young boys who thought they knew everything in the book . . .

Connie did not even think of adding her own problem to his grief and worry.

On Thursday morning he went back to the hospital, to his office.

On Thursday afternoon the children were playing on the back lawn, with Connie sitting near enough to watch them. Madie was busy inside. Scottie sat some feet away, reading. He had taken over the terrace as his right, had established himself there. John called him the man who came to dinner, and the similarity was not too funny. John acknowledged his fault in not having moved Scottie when he first became ill. "I thought he would recover enough to want to go," he confessed to Birch.

Connie saw the stranger coming around the drive before Scottie did. She had gone to lower the swing board so that Corey could swing. Grey never wanted this done, and had to be persuaded that his sister had rights, and diverted to other interests.

The man seemed to be one of the people who occasionally came into the grounds to look at "this marvelous house." As he rounded the corner of the terrace, he was looking up at the roof and the eaves. He rubbed the stones of the paving with his shoe tip. He frankly looked into the house doors and windows as he came on to where Scottie sat in his comfortable chair.

"Good afternoon, sir." He spoke pleasantly. "You have a handsome home here."

Scottie glanced across the lawn to Connie, and smiled a little at their visitor.

The strange gentleman was gazing up at the handsome lamp salvaged from the old carriage house. "Was this originally a barn?" he asked, his manner eager.

Connie, with one eye on the children, who were playing

amicably, moved up toward the terrace.

Scottie seemd to be apologizing for his pajamas, robe, and slippers. "I had a little spell with my heart a while back . . . " he was saying.

"You have a very pleasant place in which to recuperate," said their visitor. He smiled and said "Good afternoon" to Connie. He turned back to Scottie. "You know?" he said. "I think I've met you someplace. In fact, I'm sure I have."

Scottie shook his head.

The stranger sat down on the edge of one of the terrace chairs. "I bet I do know you," he said. "Let me think . . . It could have been the army—"

This drew only a growl from Scottie, who was beginning to look suspicious. "Buell . . . " mused the visitor, trying the name on his memory.

"His name is Scott," said Connie, her voice high and thin. "I am Mrs. Buell."

The man glanced at her and said something polite, then he turned again to Scottie. He was *sure* he knew him. He asked a dozen questions, where he had lived, where he had worked. . . .

As he talked, Scottie became angrier and angrier. His eyes were red, his lips set into lines of deep annoyance, his color rose. "Look, bud," he cried finally. "Hadn't you better get on your way? I never saw you before in my life. So get cracking, will you?"

Connie offered an apology. Mr. Scott had been ill, she said. The Buells were always glad to have people admire their home. Yes, it had been a barn and carriage house. She walked with the stranger to the far end of the terrace and saw him on his way. Then she would have cut down the grassy bank to join the children.

But Scottie called to her, his voice rough. "Connie!" he shouted. "Come back here!"

He had never called her by name before. Mrs. Toomey would have heard him. Cleve was working in the dining room, with the balcony doors open. . . .

"That guy was a policeman if I ever smelled one," Scottie told her when she came close. "What's going on here? You folks investigatin' me, or something?"

Connie put her fingertips on the low table. "I don't know who he was," she said. "He said—often people come in to look at the house. It is unusual . . . "

"Oh, malarkey!" Scottie cried. "I wouldn't believe you. . . . And what is the big idea . . . ? I just know this: don't bring any more fuzz around asking me questions. I've got answers for them. Sure I do! And I'm not in any mood . . . "

He got loud, he got ugly. Mrs. Toomey came out, and Cleve came down the balcony steps. Scottie threw things at both of them, the ash tray, his book— He sent a glass winging past Cleve's ears. It shattered against the house wall.

"Oh, stop this!" cried Connie sharply. "Stop this nonsense right now!"

Scottie growled something.

"You're getting yourself excited over nothing!" Connie told him. "You'll have another attack. Cleve, will you please ask Madie to come take the children upstairs? Mr. Scott should be quiet."

And the children should be safe, she thought. Grey had come running up the lawn to see what "all the yelling" was about.

Connie turned back to Scottie, who still was fuming, rolling his chair back and forth, and saying things about the police, and the ways to treat a guest. . . .

She could have answered him.

"Look," she said as calmly as she could manage. "That man was not from the police!" Should she ask him what he was afraid of?

". . . think he was," grumbled Scottie. ". . . and you called him."

She had not called him.

"I think he was exactly what he claimed to be. A person passing the house, interested in what we have done with a barn. . . ."

Scottie answered with such force, he looked so angry, his color was so bad . . .

"He could have another attack," Connie said to Mrs. Toomey.

"Yes, ma'am, he could. You think I should get him back to bed?"

"If he would go willingly." Scottie could indeed have another attack—and die. Three weeks ago Connie would have welcomed the thought, and not regretted the event. Three weeks ago she had wanted him to die.

But it was not what she wanted now. If he should die suddenly, enough things had happened, little things and big things, that people—people like John's brothers, and John himself—might suspect her of having caused the attack and Scottie's death. If it ever came out who the man was, they would *know* she was to blame.

"I think we'll all stay upstairs for a time," she told Toomey. Madie had already removed the children. "And let things be quiet for him down here."

That was on Thursday, when John might still have been at home, enjoying his "bonus" days. What if he had been there, to see Scottie's reaction to the stranger? He certainly would have asked a few questions himself. What sort of man so feared the police?

Connie tried to decide if she wished John had been at home. She still planned to talk to him; the weekend would offer her an opportunity. Today would be a heavy one for the doctor; he would come home tired. He had a heavy schedule for Friday. But on Saturday, or Sunday—

This determined upon, everything seemed to happen, and in all directions. On Friday morning, Connie did some shopping, taking Madie and the children with her. "I think they disturb Mr. Scott," she made an excuse.

They came home. Afterward, Madie said she thought the children had gone upstairs with their mother. Connie thought they were with Madie, who was going to put some clothes into the washer.

Scottie had been sitting on the terrace, wrapped in a thick robe because there was a cool breeze. Cleve had seen him there within ten minutes. Mrs. Toomey had brought the bed linens to the laundry room and stayed to chat with Madie. Connie was called to the phone before she had finished putting away the things she had bought.

Emma was in the kitchen.

Connie realized that she was not hearing the children. Madie came upstairs without them. Where were they? she asked. Where *were* they? They called, and received no answer.

Emma, Cleve, Madie—Connie—went in all directions. There simply were no children about. The lawn, and the swings—the pool fence gate was locked. The playroom—the front lawn—

Cleve brought the word. "Mr. Scott, madame," he said anxiously. "He ain't in his wheelchair."

Scottie!

Her skin pricking with fear, her neck rigid, Connie flew down the stairs. Scottie was not on the terrace, not in the guest room, the playroom—

Where had he gone? *Where* had he taken the children?

Everyone was in a panic. Everyone made excuses and offered suggestions. They called the children's names. The gardener came up to the house to help.

Connie thought she would faint, or even die. She could not breathe, she was so frightened. If that man had dared . . .

"He wouldn't go far," said Mrs. Toomey in a practical tone. "Just wearing his pajamas and them terry slippers."

"But the children!" Connie screamed at her. "If he took the *children!*"

She would call the police, she would call Birch—she even would call Dr. Buell. Surgery or no, she would tell him.

And then they heard it—Grey's high, bell-like voice—at a distance. . . .

Connie almost fell down the stairs from the deck. He was down the hill—way down— She ran, and ran, falling once and skinning her knee. Then she could see them. They *were* with Scottie! Going down along the river road. That man, and her children! Corey's yellow hair in the sunlight, Grey's sturdy brown legs . . .

The gardener was a tall man; his long strides took him swiftly down the hill.

Connie heard him say something gruffly about "not takin' the children without tellin' somebody. . . ."

And Scottie professed to be surprised. ". . . not going anywhere," he said, the picture of innocence. "Just a little walk. That's supposed to be good for a man with a heart condition."

By then she was upon them; she snatched Corey up into her arms, she grabbed Grey. . . . In her panic, of course she frightened them both. She knew that she was frightenening them, but she could not stop. Panic had whirled her up into its strong winds; she no longer could control herself. She had come to the place where she could bear no more. She was tired, and frightened. She could tell no more lies, live no more lies. Was there no way out? No place to turn? Away from this thing? This terrible thing!

Madie met her, took Corey from her arms and tried to comfort the crying children. "We just went for a walk," Grey kept saying between sobs. Corey just cried dismally.

"I'll take them upstairs," said Madie sorrowfully. "That man shouldn't-a frightened you."

"No, he should not!" said Connie angrily. "And I shall tell him so!"

"While he's comin' up the hill, ma'am," said Madie tactfully, "don't you want me to put somethin' on your knee? And your skirt's all grass-stained. . . . "

Connie took a deep, shaking breath. "I was so frightened," she confessed.

The children watched Madie wash Mommy's skinned knee and put "red stuff" on it. The ritual so familiar to themselves helped them recover from their fright.

Connie quieted, too, enough to change from her yellow skirt and blouse to a blue dress. But then she went downstairs to tell Scottie what was in her mind to tell him. She asked Mrs. Toomey to leave them alone, please.

"His walk didn't seem to hurt him none," said the nurse,

departing.

Connie closed the terrace doors and came back to Scottie. "I don't suppose I need say all the things I could say to you," she began coldly. "And I don't want to say them. Because you are leaving, and you are leaving right away."

Scottie sat in his chair and looked up at her, a half smile on his face. "That's what you have to say to me, is it?" he asked. "I've told you before, Connie. You are giving yourself away."

"Away to whom?" she demanded. "Doesn't everybody think we're crazy to have let you stay here at all?"

"They may," he agreed. "They may. And now you are making them ask what is behind all this. You've got that Beeze brother of Dr. Buell's suspicious of you. I don't guess anyone could print what he's thinking about you and me. As for the lawyer one, he's doing some investigating. I know that, too. He sent that man here yesterday to look me over and try to get some information out of me. The one he should have talked to was you. I've had a lot of training in not talking to guys like him."

Connie could only stare at him, hating every inch of him—his shiny skin, his curly hair, his sly eyes and cruel mouth.

She turned on her heel and walked to the door. "I am going upstairs, Mrs. Toomey," she said calmly, her voice clear. "Keep a close eye on Mr. Scott, will you, please?"

There *was* someone she could turn to. John. And that evening—when he came home—tired or not—she would tell Cleve that they did not want to be disturbed by any visitors, and—

Why hadn't she done this, felt this way, days and days ago?

Well—now she had the courage, now she would do it.

Somehow she managed to get through that long, long day. She ate lunch with the children and let them talk about that poor sick man downstairs. During their nap time, she rested and read in the living room, thankful when she heard rain on the deck boards and against the front windows. The children themselves would know that the wet world out of doors would prevent their play on the lawn or in the pool.

She carefully planned a dinner for John, but when he came in, she clung to him fiercely, no longer able to control herself and to keep her poise.

He held her close until her breathing calmed and her trembling ceased, his lips upon her brow, his arms about her, strong, and warm, and safe. She sighed heavily, her cheek against his breast.

Then he held her enough away to look into her face and to search her eyes. "Has there been more trouble?" he asked, his quiet tone quieting her.

"Well—" she said. "I do want to talk to you. . . . "

He nodded. "All right. Could I have a drink first?"

She tried to smile. It was a sorry attempt, but she straightened and brushed her dark hair back from her face. "Of course," she said. "I'll fix it myself."

John said he would go in to see the children; she heard them squealing and laughing. He would ask Madie, and she would tell him. Or Grey would say, "We went for a walk with the man, and Mommy thought we'd runned off."

After fifteen minutes, she heard John go down the outside stairs . . . to the terrace . . . to Scottie. . . . .

In the kitchen, Emma was being talkative. "You're a good wife to the doctor," she told Connie. "A lot of women are good mothers and housekeepers, but first of all, you are a *wife*."

For the last time, Connie thought drearily. And really not a wife at all. Not John's wife. . . .

Her fingers fumbled as she put ice into the crusher, and three of the cubes skittered across the kitchen floor. She wanted to scream and scream. . . .

She found the cubes and put them into the sink. She took her silver bucket back into the living room; she put the crystal ice into the small pitcher, squeezed a lime, poured the rum very carefully, added the sugar, her hand trembling, but the exact amount went in. She stirred and stirred the drink, set the filled glass on a small tray. . . .

She had to know what John was saying to Scottie! She had to know! She picked up the tray, but it shook in her hands. She would just go down—to tell John his drink was ready, and that dinner would be—

The stairs were sheltered by the overhanging balcony, but she threw a sweater across her shoulders against the damp wind, and went slowly down, both reluctant and anxious.

John may have asked Scottie what had happened; Connie could hear Scottie's voice—he was in the sitting room of the suite, and probably he was telling about the "policeman."

"All right," John broke in. He came out through the terrace door, and Scottie followed him, on his feet.

"I'd like to talk to my wife alone," John told him.

Scottie said something insolent. Connie's ears were ringing so that she did not hear distinctly—something like, "I don't blame you. . . . In your position, I'd like that, too."

"Look here, Scott," John said, turning on him. "Do you want me to ask Mrs. Buell right now to phone for an ambulance or a police car?"

Scottie laughed. "She wouldn't do either one."

Connie saw John's fist clench. He must not hit the man!

He did not. "Will you please wait in your room?" he said coldly. "I want to talk to my wife."

"You said that before, Doc," said Scottie, but, with a warning look at Connie, he turned back and went into the suite.

Connie went up the stairs, John close behind her. She was trembling, but she still meant to talk to him.

He had his drink. No, it was not watered down. He said, yes, they would talk, but could it wait until he had eaten dinner? His lunch had been sketchy. While he was having his drink, Connie went to tuck the children in. When she returned, John was putting the telephone back on the desk. He smiled at her, and they went in to dinner.

All right. Connie would go through the motions. She could wait. She even ate some of the chicken and the salad; John talked to her about Benny's nephew, about the work he had done that day. . .

Now and then he would glance across the table at her, his eyes concerned. Did he guess what she was thinking, how she was feeling?

Determined, of course. But in that determination, Connie was knowing a bleak foresight of what her talking to John would mean. What her telling him . . .

She would *not* go back to Scottie! That she would not do!

The dessert was a hot apple dumpling with a caramel sauce. "I thought this wet evening justified it," Connie told her husband when she saw that he was pleased.

She barely touched hers.

And John saw that.

She heard him tell Cleve to answer the telephone, and, except for a medical emergency, not to disturb Mrs. Buell and him. "Friends and family, tell them we'll call back. We don't want to be disturbed for an hour, Cleve."

"No, sir. Is Mrs. Buell feeling all right?"
"She will be."
"Yes, sir. I was sorry she was frightened today."
"Yes."
John came into the living room; he took Connie's hand and, as he would have led Corey, he led her to the deep couch. "Sit here beside me," he told her. "It is too warm, I am afraid, for a fire."
She looked at the wide hearth, and at the logs which were laid across the fire irons. "Yes," she said in a small voice.
The little white cup sat on the coffee table. There were white roses in the glass bowl, their fragrance faint but sweet throughout the room. A gust of wind blew rain against the glass. John's arm went behind her shoulders and drew her close. "The best way to get a thing done," he said, "is to start the job."
Connie nodded, her dark hair clinging to the cloth of his gray coat. He waited.
"The children?" he suggested finally. "Did something dreadful happen to them today?"
"Oh." She clasped her hands tightly in her lap. How long, how long would he let her sit here beside him?
"He . . . " she began. "Mr. Scott, you know—he took the children down the hill. Clear to the river road. It frightened me. He—" She turned, and the words blurted out. "He is not a doctor!" she said. "John, I know he is not!"
His eyebrow went up. "Yes," he agreed. "I know that, too."
She turned on the cushions so that she could look into his face. To sit in that way, she had to draw one knee up under her, a childish position. John smiled at her. The dress she wore was of coarse-woven material, a rich rose in color. It

was a simple dress, round against her throat; it left her arms bare.

"But how did you know?" she demanded, wide-eyed.

John did have a nice smile; it crinkled his eyes and spread his lips. "I've talked to the fellow," he said. "Rather, he's talked to me. The stories he told—about gun-toting doctors, and his advice that all surgeons should keep a gun handy—"

"He was fishing to see if you had a gun."

"Maybe. But he talked— Connie, I know the minute a man comes into my hospital, claiming to be a doctor, or talks as one for half an hour—I know whether he's a doctor or not."

Connie sighed and sat back against his shoulder.

"Always?" she asked.

"Always."

She nodded. She could relax, a little. John was a smart man. He knew, before she spoke, so much of what she was trying to tell him.

"*How* did you know?" she asked now, more curious than anything else.

"Oh . . . The cases he cited, the language he used. He discussed recovery rooms, and intensive-care units, as if they were dreams, ideas he might be thinking about—and you know we've had them in use for some time now. His figures on what malpractice suits cost doctors were way too high. Lord knows, they actually are high enough! He didn't know the hours nurses work these days. You should have caught that, Connie."

"I haven't been in touch for six years," she reminded her husband. "And when he sees Mrs. Toomey around for twenty-four hours . . ."

"Oh, yes. Toomey. What kind of nurse is she, Connie?"

Connie shrugged. "All right, I suppose. She hasn't had much to do."

"I wonder if she thinks he is a doctor?"

"I don't know. . . ."

"Without going into his technical lapses, he claims to be a surgeon, but he says he doesn't like vinyl drapes. He also said he got his license when he was an intern. Oh, he made all the mistakes made by a person wanting to claim his M.D. without studying for it. He . . ." John broke off and leaned forward to look into her face. "You knew he was no doctor," he said. "How?"

He was looking at her steadily, but his eyes were kind. She could say what she wanted to say. He would listen and consider each thing as honestly, truthfully told to him. He sat back, and his arm again went around her shoulders. She longed to just sit there, warm and safe, not to stir up all the ugliness, the shame, not to show him what she had been, and was.

She pushed free from him and sat erect, staring across the room, across the coffee table, and the little cup from Woolworth's, across the chairs and the table against the windows. In the glass of it she could see the room reflected—John seated on the couch, and herself beside him, the small figure of an unhappy woman, anxious, frightened, but she hoped—brave.

"I have things to tell you," she said tightly. "I don't want to tell you—but I must. And you must let me. You must not be too kind, and you must not tell me to stop."

"All right, Connie," he said quietly. "I'll listen."

He got up, went to the small bar and fixed himself a highball. He brought it back and when he sat down, his arm again went around her shoulders. He saw the tears come into her eyes. He was a most observant man.

She often had difficulty in speaking, she sometimes was incoherent, and she threatened to become excited. But she did tell him her story, going back, and back, to those high school days, and to the ignorant girl she had been.

"I didn't know a thing, John!" she cried. "I ran off with that man—that Scottie Stringer—and I married him, and I didn't know what he was, or what a man could be. I was such a fool. Even at sixteen, I was a *fool!*"

John sipped at his drink.

"He was not good to me," she continued. "And he left me after six months. I suppose that was the one kind thing he ever did. I was glad he was gone— I left the house where we had been living, and the town. Oh, John, you don't know how a cheap rooming house can smell! And then I heard that Scottie had died. He'd always said he had a bad heart. When I went home, my father showed me a clipping. I was so glad, so relieved that I didn't need further proof. I just felt that I really could forget he had ever lived. Then I studied nursing —and I met you—and you said you loved me. Suddenly life seemed to have everything to give me. I should have known— not to be proud. I should have told you about Scottie. But he was dead! He was! And you showed me how a man could love a woman and not shame her. Then Grey was born. And Corey. There was this house— And then—that awful night! He came back. He came *here!* To my house!"

"Did he hurt you, Connie" John asked, his deep voice so quiet that she answered as if continuing with her own thinking. "He threatened me—he wanted money, he said he and I could get plenty from you—and then he had this spell—and —and— Now he must leave. It isn't safe—but . . ." Her voice rose and thinned.

"I won't go with him, John. I am *not* his wife! I will have to go away, I suppose, but not with him."

"You won't go away at all," said John quietly.

She looked up at him. "But—"

"You'll stay right here," he said firmly, "as you have been doing. Loving me. Caring for my home and our family. We have never felt it was wrong, have we?"

"But, John. . . ."

He leaned forward to set his tall glass on the table. "If it was wrong," he said reasonably, "we have liked it. We shall still like it."

She smiled at him sadly. "He'll talk," she said. "People will know. Someone—Beeze, I suspect—already is sleuthing, trying to find out who he is. A day or so ago—yesterday—a man came here and asked Scottie all sorts of questions. He was furious."

"Was that when you decided to tell me about him?"

She glanced up at his face. He was grave; his question had been only curious.

"No!" said Connie tensely. "I have wanted to tell you, from the first. I did deceive you when I didn't tell you I had been married before. But since we have been married, I have kept nothing from you, John!"

His hand tightened on her shoulder.

"I wanted to tell you who he was," she said, "that first night. But I was so terrified. And now—whatever comes—I don't know that I can face what *will* come, John. He—he—" She sat with her head down. "I thought something might happen," she said. "I knew that I couldn't let him blackmail you —or me."

John's face hardened.

"But I didn't want you to fight him, either. I thought," she repeated, "I thought that something would happen. I was—I was even ready to kill him."

"So was I," said John quietly.

She gasped, looked up at him and put her fingers over her lips. "Not *you*, John! Not you."

"Oh, yes. Many times. I saw how he terrified you. I thought he probably had hurt you when he first came—and I considered ways of killing him. That he should have broken into my home, endangered my children—"

"Oh, no!" she cried. "Oh, no!" She broke into wild weeping. John drew her into his arms and held her close. "When I think," she sobbed, "when I realize what he has done to you . . ."

"I'm glad you can realize it," he said dryly. She looked up questioningly. "I can't always believe it myself," he explained. "That this man could come in here . . ."

"Did you have any idea who he was?" She sat up, wanting to see his face.

"Not when he first came, no, of course not. I would have killed him just for coming into my home and terrorizing my wife. . . "

"Only," said Connie dismally, "he's right. I am not your wife at all."

He drew her to him again. "Of course you are," he said, half laughing. "A perfect wife, loving, sweet—"

His hand stroked her hair, and it was his turn to gaze at the black mirror of the window glass, to see them seated on the couch, husband and wife.

On the day when he had married Connie, her father, an earnest little man, wanting the very best for his daughter, had told John Buell of Connie's early marriage. John would tell Connie about that, sometime. It would relieve her to know that he had not been deceived. He, too, had believed Stringer to be dead. The registrar who issued their marriage license had so marked their application without question. In a small town, things like that were known.

But now— He thought he had suspected who Scott was from the time he knew the sick man was being ugly to his wife. "Don't let that man hit Mommy!" Grey had said to his father. But even before that—perhaps. In any case, he had cared for the intruder, angry that he should have intruded, but the man was sick. And while suspicious of his identity, acknowledged or not, he had decided to keep Scott where he could watch him. He had known that something was deeply wrong; he never would have kept the patient at home so long under ordinary conditions. He had thought he could handle the man. Toomey was experienced in caring for difficult patients, psychos and alcoholics. He had thought his family was safe. His suspicions had made him ask Birch to help him. All the time, of course, he had been reluctant to acknowledge just what sort of situation he had in his home. He had tried to deny it, ignore it—certainly not to talk about it.

And he had left Connie to worry about things alone.

Now he sighed and bent his head to kiss her hair. "All this is in the past," he murmured.

"But . . ." protested Connie, stirring a little.

"Your marriage to this man," John pointed out to her, "your unhappiness in that marriage, was behind you, in the past, when I married you. And I did that because I loved you, Connie, my darling. I still love you. Just as dearly, just as warmly. . . ."

"How can you?" she asked drearily. "I lived with that awful person for six months. What must you *think* of me?"

"That I love you. I loved you when I married you. It was a wonderful sort of love—it is still wonderful."

It was. It had been.

"I know that," she said, "but still . . ."

He drew her to him so that he could kiss her lips. "I love you, darling," he said. "I'll keep saying that until you believe me. As for what I think of you— A man doesn't *think* in that sense about the woman he loves. He just—loves her." He kissed her again.

And she wept. He comforted her until she became quiet. "I'm going to be soaking wet," he complained. "All these tears."

She gulped and wiped her eyes with his handkerchief. "But there's still our marriage to think about, John," she insisted. "And our children. If I am a bigamist . . ."

He chuckled. "You'll look cute in jail," he assured her.

"It isn't funny. He just might try to put me there."

"Let him try!"

"I should have been sure that Scottie was dead," she said. "I shouldn't have—" She was completely serious about the whole thing.

"Don't you love me, Connie?" he asked.

She looked up at him with all the adoration and blind faith he often saw in Corey's eyes, and Grey's. "All right, then," he said. "That's what it is all about. That is what I want of life."

"John, darling—"

He nodded. "Now that we've got that straight, there are things that must be attended to. And we may as well talk about them now."

"First of all, you may not be a bigamist—which is an awful word to put to a little girl like you! But you may not be one."

"How can you say that? With Scottie alive, and I'm married to you?"

"I'll explain. Because there is this fact to be considered: if Scott—or Scottie—is a liar now, maybe he was one when he married you. That is one of the things Birch and his bloodhounds can look into. The man could have had an earlier marriage. If he would walk out on you, he may have walked out on some other girl. He was old enough to have had several alliances."

"But why *me?* I was only sixteen, and dumb—"

"As lovely as you are now, Connie, you must have been exquisite at sixteen. Wide-eyed—innocent, as you say—that gets to a certain kind of man."

She didn't like the picture, though she did like to think she might be free.

But the small ray of hope was soon quenched. "And if there was no earlier marriage," she said, "I'm still a bigamist."

"Then we shall handle that."

She nodded. "Yes. With all the publicity . . ." She looked upward. "And there has to be some, John!"

His fingerprints stroked the curve of her soft cheek. "There will be no publicity if I can help it," he assured her.

She sighed, believing him. He had worked other miracles. But Scottie—or someone like Irene—

"I've never thought our personal affairs should be public property," John was explaining to her. "I'll talk to Birch—"

"I thought of doing that," Connie said.

"Before you thought of talking to me?"

"No. At least, it wouldn't have been done on the same basis, John. Birch is a lawyer. I did ask him about common-law wives. If I was one, I knew I'd have some rights. But to tell you—that was a different thing. I felt so shamed before you, so dirty, so unworthy . . ."

He laughed and drew her to his lap. "You couldn't be *un-*

worthy!" he told her. "Things are not balanced that way, my darling, when a man loves a woman as I love you—as I have loved you since I first saw you. And—I thought you loved me."

"Oh, I do, I do!" She kissed him fiercely; she clung to him.

When the little storm subsided, he asked her teasingly—perhaps even jealously, "What about Scott? And your love for him?"

She shuddered.

"I don't mean today. Or even the day after you married him."

"You mean when I had a high school girl crush on him?" she asked. "Yes. I tingled, I shivered—but I didn't know what love was. No more than Corey knows such things. When I was sixteen, I wasn't one bit smarter than Corey is right now."

For a long five minutes they sat silent, comforted by their closeness to each other, and reassured. It was Connie who roused first.

"What are we going to do, John?" she asked. "We can't go on being worried. Your work— We must get him out of the house."

"Oh, he's gone," said John, as if that were a foregone conclusion.

She stiffened. She looked at him. She got to her feet and stood away so that she could look at him more directly. He began to smile.

"But—*how?*" she demanded, as if she wondered how some magician had performed a trick.

John shrugged. "It took a little time," he said modestly. "We couldn't risk the man's doing something unpleasant. I didn't even want a big row here in the house. And of course, once he was out of the house, we had to have some protection. . . ."

"But how? And when? He was down there at dinner-time."

"Mhmmmn. And while we were eating dinner—if you will remember I had the hi-fi going a little on the loud side?—while we were busy with Emma's good chicken and the wonderful apple dumpling—an ambulance came, and a police car. Mrs. Toomey and our unwelcome guest departed—for the hospital where his condition will be checked and made part of the record. Birch thought of all the angles, I believe.

"He deplored my keeping him here, but since I'd had Rinke come so he could testify as to the heart attack, and the man's care— And now Birch has secured an injunction that will keep Mr. Scott—"

"Stringer," murmured Connie.

"He's using Scott now. Anyway, this injunction, which covers several names, will keep the man from approaching us, threatening us, and so forth. Should he attempt any of that, Birch is prepared—and will say he is prepared—say it to Scott—to prefer charges because of his forced entry into our home."

"It will get in the papers," said Connie, sitting down again, looking tired.

"If it does," said John, "the papers will say something about this man having been the first husband of Mrs. John Buell."

"But—"

"We won't need to explain a thing, Connie. A lot of women have had 'first husbands.' "

She sighed and nodded. "I'll still be a bigamist, won't I?"

"There will be ways to set things right. Legal ways, I mean. The children can be adopted, and the marriage annulled. . . ."

Connie's eyes grew wide. That meant that she still would be married to Scottie, and— She jumped to her feet. "I can't bear it!" she cried. "I shouldn't beg you, but I have to beg you. I've loved you so much. . . ."

He could only stare at the small whirlwind which he had activated. "What are you talking about?" he asked, bewildered. "What— Why should you have to beg?" Then it struck him, and he began to laugh. He went swiftly to Connie and lifted her in his arms. "You're right!" he cried. "You are no smarter than Corey. I didn't mean to annul *our* marriage, you sweet idiot. I meant whatever marriage you had had with Scott. Even if he didn't have a previous one, if you were only sixteen when you married him, and didn't have your parents' consent, possibly that marriage can be annulled.

"In any case, you are my wife, and you will be. Legally, actually, lovingly, passionately."

She looked foolish, and happy, and proud, all at once. "You're a good man, Dr. Buell," she said softly.

"I love you."

"Yes. I know you do."

He tilted her chin. "Do you love me?"

She looked into his eyes, startled. "But you *know* I do!" she cried. Then a delicious, rosy color began to stain her cheeks. "And I've meant all along to keep you, too! Married or not."

He laughed. "But we are married, or will be. And the children—that will be all right, too. We'll adopt the ones we have, all legal, and the next ones—they'll be ours."

She reached for his hand. Taking him with her, she made a tour of the room, looking at things, smiling at them—the way she used to do. "I don't want to go down there now," she said, "but I am going to change everything down in the guest suite. And even up here. . . . Could I, John? Have different colors, and arrange things differently?"

"You can have anything you want," he told her. "But why? Does this room need changing?"

"I thought—to get the memory out of my mind—the picture I have of his coming in here, my fright—"

"I'll even build you a new house."

"Oh, no!" she cried. They were standing before the fireplace, and her hand stroked the rough stone. "But I don't really believe I will change anything. Scottie wasn't able to hurt me, was he? So there is nothing to forget."

14

John said that things were settled, and Connie tried to believe him. She valiantly endeavored to pick up the threads of her life. She took each of the children to the dentist; she went to a few social gatherings with John, not really enjoying them, either in prospect, or in their happening.

John wanted her to forget Scottie and all he had brought into their lives, but this was impossible for her to do—or for him, either. There were talks to be arranged with Birch. He must get the legal wheels turning to set things straight for the John Buells.

"I'm sorry," murmured Connie. "Birch has his own troubles."

"Yes, he does," John agreed. "But he says our problem has helped him to a solution of his own."

Connie looked up, her face bright with hope. He sat on his heels and squinted at the line-up of balls on the croquet court.

Scottie was in the hospital. "Will he stay there?" Connie asked on another evening, not really wanting to talk about him, but wanting even more to know where he was.

"He'd better stay there," said John grimly.

"But—"

"If he gives us any trouble, he'll be charged for entry into our home. He's been told that, quite plainly. The man has a record, Connie; he won't readily ask for anything new."

Connie wanted to believe that. "You can't keep him in the hospital indefinitely, can you?" she asked fearfully.

"Oh, no. We can't."

Then he looked up. "Of course, once out, he will need a job. To eat, to—"

"Can he get a job? What would he do, John?"

John folded his hands behind his head. He was catching the late sun, stretched out on the chaise on the terrace. "Look, my sweet," he said firmly. "These days, any man who wants a job can get a job."

"But—"

"Even a man with a somewhat bad heart. And blackmail is not going to be Scottie's source of income."

The guest suite was cleaned, and Connie was faced with her declaration that she wanted everything changed down there. She must force herself to go into the rooms and consider what she would do. Usually she welcomed the chance to coordinate curtains, bedspreads, slipcovers and accessories. She could keep busy for a month, planning, shopping, trying colors. But now she had no heart for the task. Later, perhaps, she would have. Meanwhile, the rooms could remain as they had been before Scottie's occupancy.

And Connie began to consider her continuing lassitude. She supposed it was reaction to the strain which she had been under. But it was not like her to be so "down." She should, perhaps, give in to it for a time, just lie about in the sun, rest. . . . Then, in a day or two, she would feel better.

In a day or two, she did no such thing. This went on for a week, two weeks, three . . .

Beeze and Sophia came to talk to her and John about their wedding plans. They would have a late-summer wedding, they said. Because of Connie's coloring, the bridesmaids' dresses were to be pink, and—

"Oh, wait," said Connie. "Please. I've been meaning to come to see you, Sophia. To ask you not to include me as a bridesmaid."

If any scandal should break, any at all, it could ruin Beeze's wedding.

Now he and Sophia, both, were protesting. They wanted Connie, they had planned . . .

"I know," she said, her color rising. "But I'll be at least ten years older than the other girls."

"You'll be ten years prettier and look ten years younger," Beeze told her fervently.

Connie smiled at him. "I'll believe that, but you'd better not tell the others."

"I'm a monument of tact."

John snorted. Sophia looked across at him, surprised. To her, Beeze was a monument of all that was desirable.

Connie smiled patiently. "Really, I mean it. I haven't been feeling too well—"

She had not, and she continued to feel not too well. One morning, seated at her dressing table, she was sure she had fainted, though only briefly. She didn't mention this lapse to John; she was just tired. . . .

"She looks worried about something," Emma told Cleve.

"That man that was here—he frightened her something

dreadful."

Emma agreed.

Then, a few evenings later, Connie collapsed entirely. She was dizzy, she began to cry—and she could not stop. Madie put her to bed as tenderly as she would have done for Corey.

When Dr. Buell came home, he was told, and went at once to Connie's room. She made an effort to rise, but he pressed her down. "Stay right there," he said. "Can you tell me what happened?"

"I began to cry—Madie put me to bed. I'm all right now."

"We'll see."

"Don't go planning on any of your doctors," said Connie spiritedly. "I am not sick!"

She had no temperature. She ate her dinner from a tray.

"I think it's a matter of nerves," Dr. Buell told Emma and Madie.

It was Irene—she and Birch came up the hill later that same evening, and John told them that Connie was in bed. "She's a little off her feed," he said.

"She's pregnant," Irene told him.

John turned sharply to look at her. "Who says so?" he asked.

"I say so."

"I don't think that could be true," John told her.

Irene laughed. "It's happened before. And right in this house."

"But I'd know . . . Oh, no, I think Connie is just tired, nervy—"

Birch moved toward the group of chairs on the terrace. With Irene along, he had not come up to talk business.

"Could I go up and see Connie?" his wife asked.

Both men vetoed the suggestion. She shrugged. "If she is

pregnant, visitors shouldn't be fatal."

"I tell you . . ." John began.

"I hear you," said Irene. "But why do you tell me? Weren't you there, Johnnie? And if not, would you care to guess who was?"

Birch's hand shot out; before he knew what he was about to do, he had slapped Irene's cheek. Slapped it hard.

She stepped back, her palm to her face. "Well!" she said. "I really did draw blood."

After an uneasy fifteen minutes, Birch took her home, and John immediately went upstairs. Connie was sleeping lightly, and he decided not to disturb her. Instead he went across to perform the nightly bedtime ritual with Grey and Corey. Their mother, he told them, was not feeling well.

"Did she break her leg?" asked Grey seriously.

"I don't think so. . . ."

"You'd better look," advised his son. "A broken leg is pretty bad."

He had better look.

The next morning when the telephone rang and John rose unwillingly to dress and go to the hospital, he pushed Connie back to the pillow.

"I'm all right," she told him, her gray-blue eyes misty still with sleep.

"You're fine," he agreed. "But just the same . . . And look, darling . . ." He sat beside her, took her hand in his. "This morning I want you to make an appointment with Dr. Hyndman."

Connie's eyes grew wide. Dr. Hyndman was the obstetrician. She sat up straight. "But—" she began.

He smiled at her. "You could be," he said.

Yes, she could be.

She was.

Connie herself was unbelieving, and then somewhat embarrassed. It couldn't have come at a worse time, she told John. "I mean, we *have* Corey and Grey, but . . ."

He reassured her. He was kind, but he also was being very quiet those days. Thoughtful. Even bothered.

About her? Dr. Hyndman said she was all right. There were the usual admonition about diet and exercise. There had been those orders for the other babies. Then, John had been happy, smug, ready to plan . . . talkative . . .

This time . . .

He was aware of the difference. He knew that he was being silent, and often, as Connie once told him, "away" from her, the house, the family.

Because, in spite of all he could say to himself, his fingers counted the days. Scott had come to the house in June. His coming had terrified Connie, and at the time John had suspected physical and violent assault. Now, six weeks, two months later—

"Weren't you there, Johnnie? And if not, who was?" Who *was?*

He did not want to believe what Irene had suggested to his errant thoughts. He would not believe . . .

And if he had to believe it, there should be no difference. It would not make any difference. This was Connie's child. Connie was his wife.

He loved her—dearly—and now, with a hurt intensity which he feared to express and to examine.

After ten days of this, John asked Connie if she would not like to visit her parents. She had not seen them for nearly a year. "You could take Madie and the children, or just go yourself. . . ."

"Will you go, too?"

"No. I can't get away just now. We are setting up that new resident-intern system. . . ."

He sometimes did go home with her; often he did not. If Cleve drove the big car, the trip should not be too difficult—nor unusual. But, just the same . . .

"I'll think about it," said Connie.

She did think about it. Often during that night, and again the next morning, which was Sunday. Returning from church, she asked him unexpectedly, "Are you sending me away?" Her tone was quiet.

But it startled John, and his hands jerked on the wheel. "What do you mean?" he asked, almost angrily. Perhaps he was angry, though he seldom let himself show anger.

Connie clasped her white-gloved hands together in her lap. "I thought," she said, head down, "that you might think it better to send me away until we can be legally married."

He made a gruff sound in his throat. "I only suggested . . ."

He went on talking, and she listened, with part of her attention. But her main stream of thought was upon herself. She—she could not *bear* the thought which had, during the night, come to her. She could not endure the idea that she could be losing John.

Not for something she herself had done, or failed to do. But because he had lost his faith in her. She could not live with such a thing in her life. There would be no life. . . .

In Iowa, and Minnesota, and Illinois, lately, the farmers were engaged in raising a strange new crop. They planted whole fields in sunflowers, and as harvest approached, such fields were a beautiful sight to see. The tall green stalks, the great yellow and orange flowers—small suns, each one, that turned always to face the greater sun in the heaven—a stately ballet as the day progressed.

Except when the summer became too hot and the ground too dry. Then the golden disks no longer turned to the sun. The green stalks became stiff, and the heads would not move their necks. To follow the light . . .

". . . you're to do as you choose," John said, as he turned the car wheels into their own road.

Connie made no comment. She would go away if he wanted her to.

That afternoon, Beeze and Sophia came to the house; later Birch and Irene joined them. Everyone, including the children, took gratefully to the pool—except Connie. She sat in a chair and watched the fun; once she went to the kitchen for cold drinks and things to eat—fruit, crackers, cheese. For the children there were cookies, which the men helped eat. Beeze brought a stack of these over when he came to sit beside Connie.

"What's got into our Johnnie?" he asked her idly. "He can't really be carrying the world on his shoulders. Or can he?"

"He isn't pleased that I am having a baby," said Connie, not thinking about what she said.

"Are you?" Beeze turned to look at her.

"Didn't Irene tell you?"

"I don't talk to Irene, nor listen when she talks."

"Maybe you should. She knew before I did that a baby was coming."

"Gee whiz! When did all this happen?"

Connie smiled at him, and he flushed. "I meant, when did Irene say . . . ?"

"I'm past the second month," she said gently. "And Irene—well, you're right. It doesn't matter what she said."

Beeze thoughtfully ate his last cookie, reached for Connie's glass, and drank her lemonade. "Two months," he mused. "I guess the old boy—John, you know?" He glanced at her. "I guess he thinks the kid may be our late friend Scott's. Anyway, he could be afraid it is. . . ."

Connie jumped to her feet, and she screamed a little at Beeze. That he should dare to say such a shocking thing, to say it . . . "Don't make jokes like that, Beeze!" she cried.

He shrugged. "Who's joking? I don't know of anything else that would put John into such a plaster cast. That man's troubled, girl. He's *troubled!*"

Yes. John was troubled. But—

"It just isn't true," she cried tensely. "You can't believe it!"

Beeze reached for her hand. "Look, my sweet," he said. "You know how fond I am of you. But when that character showed up here—and you were so frightened, so devastated—we all thought the guy had raped you."

"John didn't think so!"

"I'm afraid he did, Connie. I am sure he thinks so now."

"Well, he's wrong! You're all wrong!"

"Can you prove that?"

"I'll prove it," Connie promised grimly.

"You'd better."

Connie sat down again in her chair. "It might not do any good, Beeze. If he can think . . ."

"He can think Scott did it, or he can think the child is his. But he doesn't *know*, Connie. That's what is bugging the man."

"He could ask me," she said sorrowfully. "Don't you think he would believe me?"

"He'd want to, sweetheart. He would want to."

"Then I must prove it. . . ."

Beeze shrugged. "If you can. . . ."

If she could. Connie must find a way. There must be a way!

That evening, after the callers left—and the next morning, the next evening when John came home from the hospital—

Once the doubt had been born in his thoughts, against his will, it quickly grew to Gargantuan proportions, a giant not to be vanquished by reason.

John knew his constant companion.

Connie saw the monster, and others came to see it, Beeze particularly. This was something which John—and Connie—were going to have to live with, though neither wanted it in their home.

Where there had been love, warmth, and joy, now there were symbols only of those things. A swift kiss on his wife's cheek as he left the house, the courtesies of an innately courteous man. . . . Those gestures were not enough—for either of them.

Connie strove desperately to end the nightmare. Over and over she considered her situation. John, she told herself, could not believe the child she carried was not his.

But if he did believe that, and she would lose him . . .

She could.

He might think she had been raped.

He might even think, knowing who Scott was, that she had willingly . . .

Oh, the whole thing was a nightmare, not to be endured—nor allowed to continue.

Connie loved John, she was his wife, and she wanted his love, his faith in her. This child certainly was coming at an awkward time, but it was *his* child; he must know that it was!

Even if he wanted to believe that it was, he still must *know!* Their marriage had always been based on faith, and that was what had to be restored.

Connie, with Dr. Hyndman's help, was feeling better; her determination gave her added strength. Midweek, she dressed in a straight frock of beige linen, knotted a blue and lavender scarf at the throat, and told Madie that she was going into the city. Oh, yes, she felt all right. She had several things to attend to. She suggested a treat for the children's lunch, and things they could do. Then she drove away.

Her plans, made after hours of thinking about them, were of the simplest. She would find Scottie. She would make him tell John. . . . She was confident that she could do both things; she knew the man and his ways all too well.

She went to the hospital where John had installed him, and she was not very surprised to have the Sister at the desk tell her that Mr. Scott had checked out three days before. A.D.A. —against the doctor's advice.

"We can't really prevent this, Mrs. Buell," she said ruefully.

"I understand. I don't suppose he told you . . . ?"

"Where he was going? No, he didn't. Dr. Buell thinks we'll have him back, or at least hear."

Connie thought they would certainly hear from Scottie. He

would want money, and his nature was such that the best way for him to get it would be to hit the Buells again.

Yes, he would come around. Perhaps in person, perhaps by telephone, perhaps even through an ad in the newspaper. He had used to read the PERSONAL ads—for lost heirs, and those put in by people in grief or trouble. Connie herself might insert such an ad.

"Information of profitable interest available to W. S. Stringer." She would give a blind address.

She had no intention of giving Scottie money, but she must find him.

John must have known he had left the hospital, but he had said nothing, not wanting to worry her. Perhaps Connie should tell him what she was trying to do.

He would refuse to let her go through with it. He wanted her protected from all contact with Scottie. He would deny the need for her to prove anything to him.

Thoughtfully, Connie went back to her car. She should have a fitting for her bridesmaid dress. She still did not think she should be in the bridal party, though Sophia was insistent, and she didn't want another "sister-in-law" at cross purposes.

Sister-in-law. Irene. She and Scottie . . . That guy could get at the Buells through Irene. Or . . .

Connie was a careful driver, usually, but that morning she took a few chances to speed her way back to the Buell property, and she brought her car to a bucking stop before Birch's pretty little home.

"Connie?" asked Irene, coming to the front door.

Connie nodded, smiling. "Yes. I wanted to see you."

"You drove . . . ?"

"Oh, I've been in the city. But I wanted to see you and ask you—"

Irene stepped back to let her visitor precede her into the house. Connie was excited. Her eyes were huge, her color high.

"What about lunch?" Irene asked uncertainly.

Connie looked at her watch. "It's not quite twelve. And I do have something to ask you, Irene."

She would have to tell her enough of the sordid matter—more than John would approve telling Irene. But Connie did tell her, reminding her of Scottie, and his three-week occupancy of the guest suite. Then she told of her pregnancy—which Irene had guessed. "Cleverly," Connie added, watching the slender, redheaded woman. Irene wore blue denim shorts and a white blouse. A bright blue ribbon drew her hair to the back of her neck.

Connie took a deep breath and plunged on. "The thing is," she said quickly. "John is acting in a way about this pregnancy to make Beeze guess he is wondering if Scottie—the night he broke into our house, you know—to wonder if he might have, well, raped me, and—and—"

"He'd still be responsible for any child you would have while his wife, Connie. That's the law, I think."

Connie shook her head. "The thing is—the baby *is* John's, and I don't want him to think—"

"Men think what they want to think."

"Not John. But if he has any doubts—well, I want to find Scottie, and in some way prove to John—"

"It might be dangerous to give him any ideas that he could use for blackmail. There's a no-good guy of the first water, Connie. He'll do anything."

Connie nodded. Scottie would. And she had been right to come to Irene for help.

"I thought you might be able to help me find him."

Irene laughed. "Because I'm a no-good gal?" she asked.

Connie shook her head. "Irene, please . . ."

"All right. All right. You want help. You say you need help."

"I thought you might know how to go about finding him. I thought of a newspaper ad. . . ."

"Yes. And there are people who trace people. That costs money."

Connie nodded. "It's a matter of our marriage, Irene," she said earnestly.

"Scott didn't rape you?"

"Of course not!"

Irene's eyebrows went up. "Happens all the time. Well, let's see. You know, I think you're a nice kid, Connie, and I respect John Buell, even if he did throw us out when he married you."

"That was my fault. I was afraid I couldn't learn to be his wife with others in the home."

Irene stared at her. "You . . . ?" she repeated, then she laughed. "You know? That never occurred to me. I thought maybe you were jealous—or that John didn't trust his brothers. . . ." She examined this new concept and seemed to accept it.

"I'll try to help you, Connie," she said at last. "Birch would approve of my doing it. Say! Why don't we ask Birch to help you? He's smart!"

"I know he's smart," said Connie. "The trouble is, he agrees with John and Beeze—that Scottie may have—"

Irene got up from the couch, went to the kitchen and brought back two cups of coffee. "There's no hurry about this, is there?" she asked, sitting on the couch again.

"Yes, there is," said Connie. "John is tearing himself to

pieces, wondering, worrying. That isn't good for his work. And it isn't good for me. I want this pregnancy to be a happy time, as it was with Grey and Corey."

"They're cute kids."

"Yes, they are. And this one—it means a *lot* to me. That he should be happily loved, from the first."

Irene nodded. "I'd say," she began, speaking slowly, "that John loves you, Connie."

"I'm sure he does."

"Isn't that enough?"

"It might be. Though I, too, want him to be sure."

"What if you can't prove this? I mean, if we'd find the man, we couldn't make him say he didn't, just by *asking* him."

Connie sat thoughtful. "It wouldn't work, would it?"

"No. It wouldn't."

Connie sighed. "If I can't prove it, I shall have to live with the thing," she said.

"Me, I'd tell John Buell what the truth was, and say he could believe me or else." She looked across at her visitor. "But that wouldn't be your way, would it?"

Connie smiled wanly.

Irene jumped to her feet. "All right. I guess I had better help you—if I can. D'you have any ideas of how to go about hunting this Scott?"

"I thought maybe—if he had talked to you about his interests, you know, or places he knew, or people . . ."

"I talked to him a time or two. How about that nurse you had?"

"Toomey. Yes, that's a lead."

"If I read him right, he'll be getting in touch with you."

For money. Yes. Scottie would get in touch.

"Look," said Irene compassionately. "Don't look so scared. This is your baby, whoever its father might be."

"It is John's baby," Connie said firmly. "It cannot be anyone else's."

"After it is born, aren't there blood tests and things . . . ?"

"Yes, but it is important for me—for John—to know now! As I told you, it is important for him to share this with me."

"I'll believe you. But I'm thinking . . . Look. Suppose we find this guy—this Scottie. How would you get him to testify?"

"There must be ways," said Connie firmly. "Oh, he wouldn't be big-hearted and get me out of a jam. No! But I thought you— Men fall for you, Irene."

Irene looked down at her shorts and at her bare feet. "Old glamor girl, eh?"

"They *do* fall for you." Connie looked ready to weep.

"All right, all right," said Irene. "But we gotta find the guy first. And then . . ."

"If you find him, he'll tell you. Not in so many words, of course. But if—say—he wanted to make out with you— Isn't that the term?"

Irene grinned at her. "Then I'm supposed to ask him just how tied up he is with you, huh?"

Connie flushed. Irene sat down again, her chin on her fist. "He came here once, he might hang around the neighborhood—and I might see him. He'd be mooching, wouldn't he?"

"Sure to be," said Connie. "He calls it promoting."

Irene looked up at her. "You do know him, don't you?"

"Too well. I thought maybe you'd hear about him—even if he didn't come here to the house. Don't you go to drive-ins and those restaurants down on the river road?"

"Are you talking about Cliff Adams?" asked Irene, her face cold.

Connie flushed. "He is exactly the sort of person who could find Scottie. Scottie would approach such a man. I know he gets around—"

"And you know he hangs around here, too, don't you?" Irene demanded.

"Oh, Irene!" Connie was distressed. "I had to get help somewhere."

"I'll say you were pretty smart to figure out where to get it, too," Irene agreed. "And you're right. Cliff is exactly the one who could locate a chap like your late freeloader. Him and the police."

"We'll leave the police till later."

"But you do mean to locate the guy, don't you?"

"I want to, very much."

"I still can't think what good it's going to do you, unless you're ready to buy his testimony. Of course if you'd file a charge of rape, and the man was arrested, I suppose he'd deny it."

Connie sat shaking her head. "That would be awful," she said.

"Yes, it would be. But—the trouble is, Connie, I have promised Birch to be a good girl and not see Adams any more. I've been working on the good-girl bit, and now . . ."

"Birch would want you to help me in this."

"Why didn't you go straight to him?"

"I should have, I suppose. Or maybe even to Beeze. Birch already knows the whole situation. You and Beeze don't. But maybe—" Should she tell him without talking to John? Should she?

Irene saw how distressed she was. "Let's go talk to Birch,"

she said. "I'll call him. Maybe we can have lunch with him."

"His office would be better." Connie looked very tired and frightened.

"All right. His office. I'll call him."

"He might even get Beeze. . . ."

Irene went to the phone. Connie leaned back in her chair and closed her eyes. She thought she might faint. . . .

It took an hour for Irene to dress and to drive Connie's car into the near suburb where Birch had his offices. She thought Connie should eat something, but Connie shook her head. "I'm all right."

"You look like a sick cat."

"Oh, that's a charming picture."

"On you, it will get you far, especially with the Buells."

Connie took a deep breath. Birch already knew the whole story; he already was working on handling Scottie. The new element was to get the man. . . .

Birch's offices were new; he had been in them for less than a year. The building was in the Williamsburg style, of red brick with white window trim. Ready to go into the wide white door, Connie drew back. "It won't work," she told Irene. "There's no use bothering Birch."

Irene turned to stare at her, then she seized her arm. "Oh, no, you don't!" she cried. "You got me here—I called Birch, and he was not at all pleased—to be *bothered*. But when I told him *you* had a problem—you're going in and tell him about it honey-chile. Believe me, you are!"

"All right, then," said Connie meekly.

The hall was white-paneled, with paintings hung at intervals. Birch's offices were to the right. A receptionist welcomed them and said they were to go right in. "In" was a large corner room with a soft green carpet, small-paned windows curtained in creamy net, with rich green side draperies. There was a large desk set across the corner, a couple of brown leather chairs, a big couch of black-green wool. There were good prints on wide mats, framed in narrow walnut molding. It was a bright, pleasant room, and Birch met them kindly. He was sorry that Connie had a problem, he said. Had the girls eaten lunch? He could have sandwiches sent in, and some iced tea.

"Later, maybe," said Irene, giving him what was meant to be a warning look.

But just then Beeze charged in, demanding to know what was up. He stopped short at seeing Connie and Irene. What was this? he asked. A family conference? Where was John?

"This is about John," Connie told him, speaking in a small, thin voice.

Beeze turned to stare at her. "Look," he cried. "We don't have family conferences without John. Me, yes. Irene, certainly. Even you, maybe, Connie, but *not* without John!"

"All right," she agreed. "Then this is about me."

For another minute, Beeze stared at her, then he sat down in the chair which faced Birch's desk. ". . . beats me," he muttered.

Birch moved some papers which he had on his desk. "Suppose," he said mildy, "we let Connie tell us about the problem she thinks she has."

Everyone turned to look at her where she sat in the precise center of the long couch. She was like the crayon portrait of a young woman, a pastel. Her dark hair was a soft blur, her blue-gray eyes a smudge in her pretty face, the scarf at her throat, her round bare arms, and her hands clasped together in her lap. When she spoke, it was indirectly at first; she fumbled a little; she smiled once or twice, faintly, and once she shed a tear—but she told what her problem was. "Beeze knows about it," she concluded, her voice trembling. "What I think we need to do is to find Scottie and get proof for John—"

Beeze shifted in his chair. "How you goin' to do that?" he asked.

"I can," Connie assured him confidently. "I know that man better than you do."

"Connie . . ." said Birch warningly.

She glanced at him. "I think I must tell him, Birch. Or you can."

He nodded. "Yes. That might be better."

It was better—his impersonal tone and manner, his legal phrasing. Connie could sit back and do no more than listen. Birch's neat, mustached face showed no emotion, but every expression crossed that of his younger brother—shock, anger, pity— Once or twice he erupted into a word of protest and profanity. Irene sat fingering the little glass beads of her green earring.

"How'd you get away with it?" she asked at last.

"She thought the man was dead!" Birch told his wife sharply.

"Didn't John know . . . ?"

"That she had been married? Yes. Not that Scott, this man who turned up at their house and had a heart attack, was the man."

"Then he came . . ."

"Of course. To blackmail."

"That's why she was so terrified?"

"He seems to be a dangerous man. I believe we all decided that. We thought he had hurt Connie—she had a bruise on her arm. She was in a real panic—"

"I was sure he had raped her," said Beeze, getting up to walk around the room.

"John may have thought so, too," said Connie, her voice whispering. "Though I didn't know that until—until we discovered that I was pregnant."

"*Did* he rape you?" asked Birch, his face intent. "I think we have to know that."

"No," said Connie. "He might have had it in his mind to try it. He—he did put his hands on me, and I struggled with him—he had this heart attack—"

Birch made a notation on his big pad of yellow paper. "I believe you," he said.

"I think John wants to believe that, too," said Connie.

"But . . . ?" asked Beeze.

"Yes, Beeze. He has that nagging doubt you and I talked about."

Beeze looked sorry that he had ever put the thought into Connie's mind. "You know?" he said, attempting to correct the error, "I believe old John will talk himself into believing the kid has to be his."

"Oh, I think he will, too," said Connie readily.

"Then what's your problem?"

"I want him to know that now. This is a tender time for us. . . ."

"She means her pregnancy," explained Irene.

"Yes," agreed Connie. "I do mean that. You'll see, Beeze."

And the man blushed. Even Connie laughed to see that phenomenon. Then she turned shyly to Birch. "I hope you and Irene will know about it, too," she said.

Now everyone was confused. Irene took off her earring, dropped it, bent over to recover it. Birch stacked some envelopes on his desk and looked hard into the wastebasket. Beeze went over to the window, pushed the thin curtain aside, and stared out into the street.

"I wonder, Connie," said Birch gruffly, "what you will find to say to this man Scott, if we do find him. Do you have some plan?"

"No," she said calmly, "but I'll say something."

"I believe you will," Birch agreed. "I'm seeing a new girl here today."

"Do you think we can find him, Birch?"

"Oh, we'll find him. He'll hit John for money—or you—"

"He had better stay away from Connie," growled Beeze.

"Yes, he had better. Then—we'll publish notices of divorce proceedings, should a divorce be necessary."

"Won't that take time?"

"Yes, it probably will drag out. Meanwhile . . ."

"Meanwhile," cried Beeze angrily, "he can't get away with this!"

"He's an awful man," Connie whispered.

"I was talking about John," Beeze to her.

"Oh, no," Connie protested. "It's not that way at all. He's just horrified—for me, Beeze. To think . . ."

"Have you tried telling the guy you were not raped?"

"I would tell him—if he asked me. I'd tell him the baby has to be his."

"Wouldn't he believe you, Connie?" Birch asked.

"He'd want to, Birch."

Irene saw her husband nod, and she saw the gravity of his expression. "Connie came to me for help," she spoke up, "because she thought Cliff Adams might be able to locate this character."

Beeze looked startled. "Two of a kind, eh?"

"No," said Irene sharply. "But they both spend lonely hours in bars. For their own reasons, in bars maybe near our place."

"If you think he could help . . ." suggested Birch.

"I think he might. But I promised you to be done with Cliff."

"Could you get his help on that basis?"

She smiled. "He won't like it."

"I'll bleed later," said her husband dryly.

It took a week or ten days, and Connie was getting impatient. Irene told her that the man, that Scottie, would come around. As it happened, she was with Cliff when he actually appeared. They were parked in her car at one of the river road restaurants. Scottie came up from behind them. "Isn't your name Buell?" he asked Irene, leaning into the car.

"I thought I would faint," she told afterward. "Me!"

But she had not fainted. She and Cliff, between them, had talked to Scottie; they bought him a beer, and another one. They offered to take him anywhere he might be going. That destination was a shabby motel off a state road. They visited, and Cliff said he'd be seeing Scottie again. . . . Did he like to fish? Cliff knew where he could borrow a boat.

It was only a half-date, but at least Scottie was located. Birch was told, and Beeze, who also was cautioned to keep his mouth shut and not to take things into his own hands.

"You're not going to let Connie go in on that man alone?" Beeze demanded.

"No. She's going with Adams. And maybe Irene."

"When?"

"Tomorrow."

"What if he suspects something?"

"He may, once he sees Connie. If he runs, we'll nab him. This time the police will see that he is kept where we want him."

The next morning, Irene in slacks and striped shirt, Adams dressed like her, in brown slacks instead of green, in a yellow striped shirt instead of a red one, with Connie discreetly behind them, approached Scottie's motel room door, knocked, identified themselves, and were told to "Come in, come in!"

Scottie was on the rumpled bed, one of the chair cushions propped behind his shoulders. The TV was going full blast; Cliff turned it off. By then he had been briefed on his role in the game being played. He might still have thought he was doing his part to help Irene, and that she would be grateful—or he might just have liked playing the part.

When Scottie saw Connie, he cursed and started to get out of bed. Cliff told him to "Rest easy, brother. We want a word with you."

Scottie looked balefully at Connie, who had sat down on the edge of the low table. In a green and white checked jumper dress, snowy blouse and flat shoes, she looked like the nice, small-town girl she was.

"What do you want?" he asked grumpily. Then he looked at Cliff. "Are you hired by the Buells?" he demanded.

"My only pay check comes from the airline," Cliff told him. He leaned against the closed door.

"All right, Connie," said Irene. "You said . . ."

That she would find something to say. Yes. And she must make what she said believable. Not only to Scottie, but to Irene and this Cliff Adams. She rather liked Cliff. Beeze said he was hard-nosed in a way that the Buells were not. Ethics and manners got in the way for people like the Buells.

But Adams . . .

Connie glanced at him, then rose and took a step toward the bed. For a minute she was back in the old rooming houses which she had known with Scottie. There was the same litter of dirty glasses, rumpled sheets, discarded clothing, the same smell.

She lifted her head. "I wanted to find you, Scottie," she said in her clear voice. "To tell you that I am ready to acknowledge my marriage to you. You needn't sneak around and watch me any more."

Adams was watching her. Irene had her hand over her mouth. Scottie just peered at her with narrowed, suspicious eyes.

"What do you mean *acknowledge?*" he asked.

"What the word means, Scottie. I am ready to join you. Here, or in some other place we can find. I'll get a job, and we'll manage somehow with the children. I know there are day nurseries . . . or you could take care of them while I work."

"What're you talking about?" cried Scottie. "Buell's got money—"

"He has money, but if I am not married to him, I have no claim on that money."

"And you'd be dumb enough to give it up, too."

"Dumb or not, the children and I—"

"Oh, no, you don't!" cried Scottie. "Those kids are his."

"Yes, but they are mine, too, and I'd want to have them with you and me."

"You're crazier than a pet coon!" shouted Scottie, getting out of bed. He looked terrible, and smelled worse. Connie put a steadying hand on the dresser edge while he paced around the room, voicing his shock and his frenzied protest. She was a crazy woman, he said. This was not what he had in mind—

when he told her—

"But I have the children," Connie reminded him, when he paused, gasping for breath. "And there is another child coming. I am two months pregnant."

Scottie came toward her. Irene looked appealingly at Adams, who nodded.

"Listen to me, you dumb broad!" Scottie shouted. "You're not going to saddle me with three kids. And you besides!"

Connie did not retreat. "But I thought," she said, "if I am married to you, any children I have would legally be yours. . . ."

"The hell with *legal!*" screamed Scottie. "They sure as the devil are *not* mine!"

"No," said Connie coolly, "they are not yours."

"And you can't make any claim on me!" Scottie added. "I haven't done more than talk to you in ten years, and more!"

Connie took a deep breath. She turned toward Cliff Adams. "I think we can go now," she said softly. "You heard what Mr. Stringer said. You can be a witness. . . ."

Scottie again came charging toward her, but he stopped before he actually touched her. "Witness to what?" he demanded.

"We can go back to Dr. Buell now," said Connie, as if Scottie had not spoken, "and tell him that he can go on with the things he already has planned to do. Mr. Stringer will make no trouble."

"You can tell Birch," said Irene, "but let me tell John. I just have to tell that man!"

Connie nodded, unable to say a word more. When they were back in Cliff Adams' car, she had a bad case of the shakes. "We'll take her home," said Irene efficiently, "and then go tell Birch."

"Me?" asked Cliff, laughing.

"You," said Irene.

"I thought you wanted to tell the Doctor . . ."

"We'll do that, too. Later."

"Yeah," said Captain Adams. "Later."

Connie spent the rest of the day recovering from doing what Irene described to John as a tremendous job. "As cool as the daiquiris she makes you, she had that Scott character running like a whipped dog."

When John returned to his home that night, it was to find Grey and Corey playing on the lawn, their mother in pink linen, cool and smiling. He got out of his car, his jacket hooked on one finger; he greeted the children, then came on to Connie, who was waiting for him, smiling.

He looked down at her for a long minute, then he put out his arm and drew her to him. His kiss was long and warm. "Gee whiz!" he cried boyishly. "I've needed that all day."

Connie rubbed her cheek against his arm. Now she fully knew what she had been missing.

Grey was tugging at his father's coat. "Daddy, *Daddy!*" he cried insistently. "Do you know what?"

John turned. "No," he said. "Of course not. What do you know?"

"We're going to have another baby!" said Grey importantly. "Not for quite a time, but when the Easter bunny comes. . . ."

"Easter bunny!" Corey repeated rapturously.

"Well, what do you know?" asked John, sitting on his heels. He glanced up at Connie. "Fix me a drink, will you, sweetheart, while the kids and I think up a name for this new baby?"

"You think I don't want to be around?" she asked.

"We'll tell you."

She laughed. "I hope."

"Grey wants to name it Cleve," John reported when he joined her on the terrace.

"And Corey, I suppose, suggested Winnie the Pooh."

"No, the Easter bunny stuck with her."

"Oh, me. And what ideas did you have, Dr. Buell?"

John's hand stroked her soft hair. "I want Christina," he said.

Connie's eyes flew to his face.

"My mother's name," he agreed, "for my daughter."

Connie sighed. He could feel her do it, and his arm tightened about her shoulder. "If it's a boy," he said, "we'll save the name until a daughter comes around."